STARSOULS

AUTHOR

JOHN P NOONAN

J.P. NOONAN

STARSOULS

J.P. Noonan is an Apartment Maintenance Manager, and has been in the apartment maintenance field for over 30 years. He started his favorite hobby of writing, before his youngest child was born in 1997. He has published twelve children's rhyming books since that time.

This science fiction novel Starsouls came to John's thoughts on January 15th, 2014, while staring at the moon and stars on his back porch.

He felt it was a message from the stars, as it filled his thoughts in every detail. John started writing this novel on that night and finished on Father's Day June 15th, 2014. He wrote a couple hours every night after work and family. He wrote Starsouls in six months exactly, and typed the whole novel E.T. style, only typing with two index fingers.

STARSOULS

SELF PUBLISHED BY JOHN P NOONAN

Copyright 2014 @ Library of Congress

The cataloging-in-Publication Data is

On file at Library of Congress

Reg. # TXu 1-929-729

ISBN # **978-0-692-28187-1**

Book design by John P Noonan

Cover design by Ryan J Noonan

Alien face created by Bere' Coshin

Printed in the United States of America

"The Gathering"

Adam was driving his Ford pickup along an old familiar winding road. The rock group Super Tramp was playing the Logical Song on the dashboard radio. Around one more bend to the local watering hole called Gillian's.

Gillian's is a popular hangout for locals and N.A.S.A. astronauts, about five miles down the road from the John F. Kennedy Space Center, Florida. As his truck pulls in the gravel parking lot, the music from the bar drowns out his truck radio, as he shut down his motor.

He steps out of the truck and enters the bar for a final civilian gathering with his comrades. Adam and his friends are United States Astronauts. Adam is a Mission Specialist, with seven flown shuttle missions under his belt. A Mission Specialist is a N.A.S.A. astronaut assigned to a shuttle crew with mission-specific duties. They have a free last night together before they go into a ten-day quarantine in the morning for a special N.A.S.A. mission.

For a few days before launch, the astronauts are isolated to make sure astronauts don't get sick with a cold, or other disease during their mission flight.

The astronauts usually get a physical exam called the "L-10," ten days before launch. The exam includes lab tests to make sure they're not already sick. After this time, N.A.S.A. limits astronauts contact with other people. The real quarantine starts seven days before launch. So as Adam enters, he is greeted by Maurice, one of his comrades.

"Well, look at what the wind blew in," said Maurice as he greeted Adam.

Maurice is a Mission Commander, who has successfully commanded three shuttle missions. A Mission Commander handles overall mission success, and the safety of crew and spacecraft, also pilot in command of spacecraft during launch, trans-lunar coast, and earth return coast.

"Hey buddy," Adam replies. "Where is the rest of the crew?" "Over around the corner of the bar, we have a table over there."

"I will guide you," said Maurice. As the two walks through the crowded bar where they are well known by the locals. As they walk, they are patted on the back with well-wishers saying, "Good luck on your mission, and may God bless you."

Adam is the comedian of the crew. Every time he hears someone say, "God bless you," his answer is, "Thanks, but I didn't sneeze." As the two turn the corner they see Malone, Eve and Jeremiah, sitting at the table with drinks. Malone and Eve are International Mission Specialist, and Jeremiah is a Flight Engineer. Same as a Mission Specialist but may have payload-specific duties assigned by home agency.

A Flight Engineer is a Mission Specialist with additional responsibility of assisting the pilot and Commander. The Flight Engineer also keeps track of information from the I.S.S. and calls out milestones.

Maurice yells to the bunch, "Hey look who I found." Eve yells over the crowd noise, "Come join us for a nightcap big boy," referring to Adam.

So, the whole crew is together, chatting about the big mission and having fun.

Eve starts off the conversation saying, "Hey guys, how about this big space mission we are about to embark on."

Then Jeremiah chimes in, "Yeah, this international mumbo jumbo of different astronauts from different religions, races and creeds, all joining together on a unified spacewalk. Also, hand in hand for the sake of peace."

Adam then says, "Hey, hey, calm down, this mission is to show solidarity of space travel accomplished by man himself, to show how space travel requires no special race, religion, origin or color of someone's skin to succeed."

Maurice adds, "Yes this will be a wonderful mission that will make the history books. Seeing United States astronauts' hand in hand with Russian, French, Canadian, European, Japanese and Chinese astronauts, spread across the international space station for the entire world to see."

Malone finishes the conversation with, "This will be epic." Adam looks at the pictures of all the former astronauts proudly framed all along the pub walls.

He nudges Maurice, and says, "You know, it's an honor to be in this group of people, being surrounded by what you can call our forefathers on the walls."

Maurice replies, "You know Adam as well as me, these stripes weren't just handed to us. We worked hard to get here, and this is not a job for the meek."

Adam replied, "Your right man, but it feels good on this ride of life for me." Maurice smiled as the two saluted their drinks together.

Eve turns to Jeremiah and says, "You know I don't have much experience doing space walks. I am a little nervous about this mission in a few days. What about you?"

Jeremiah replied with, "You know, if I remember back to when I was young, and my dad took me to train on a bicycle for the first time, boy was I nervous. Especially the first time he let go, and I was freewheeling on my own. This mission reminds me of that."

"All the training underwater, tethering on that wire for a lifeline, and to think it's going to be real this time, in the vast perils of space. I'll tell you, I may seem confident on the outside, but I feel like that little boy inside, although I'll never let them see me sweat."

All at once, the bartender yells to the crowd in the bar. "Hey, before everyone leaves tonight, let's pay homage to our hometown hero's, our decorated men and woman of our military forces."

"They are sitting over there in the corner, so let's sing the "Star Spangled Banner." One patron starts off, "Oh say can you see," and another, "By the stars early light," then the whole bar joins in, and the song is born, being sung so proudly. After the song is over, everyone starts cheering, whistling, hooting, and hollering while enjoying themselves. The band played, everyone was dancing and singing with the band, with drinks sliding across the bar.

It was wall to wall packed, mostly because of the five comrades being in the bar. The locals like to gather at the watering hole to get a glimpse of the real-life space heroes.

This is one reason ordinary people of all kinds, come to the area of The Kennedy Space Center in Florida. This tavern has been a favorite place for astronauts to get together before their launches, since the early sixties. Steve Hanson, owner of the local watering hole has pictures all over the bar, with famous astronauts of the past.

The crew themselves were enjoying a couple drinks together. Not like the patrons all around them. They were getting so soused; they are approaching the astronauts like they are movie stars.

Eve turns to the guys and says, "Guys, I think our friends are harmlessly getting too friendly, so let's mosey on out of here while the times are happy, and everyone is feeling good."

Maurice replies with, "Ok crew, let's all salute to a great mission at hand by having one last drink together."

All the astronauts gather around Eve, and toast for a safe and successful mission, they were about to take.

Adam spoke up in his "John Wayne" voice and says, "Let's do this for all the great space cowboys that saddled up and rode their rockets into the history books." The rest of the crew yells, "To all the space cowboys," and gulps their last drink together.

The crowd hears the astronauts salute, and they all salute the astronauts. "Three cheers for our five astronauts," someone yells!

Well, it's getting late and as the crew parts from the bar, Adam yells out of nowhere, "Jeremiah was a bullfrog." Then the entire bar yells, "He was a good friend of mine."

So, another song is born for everyone to sing, as Jeremiah gives Adam a little punch in the arm as a pay back, all in fun.

They were laughing out the door. They all headed to their vehicles. Adam drove back to The Kennedy Space Center with a David Bowie song called, "Space Oddity," playing on his radio.

When he reaches his destination like his comrades, he will be quarantined, and kept separate from everyone until the actual launch morning. The next time he sees his partners, he can go over the mission, right after the meeting in the morning.

Then he will have a final breakfast with them before the launch.

The other four astronauts headed back to the space center also. They were all driving their vehicles, one behind the other to their base station. Things eventually quieted down at Gillian's, as the patrons eventually all went home, and as the night came to an end.

"The Press"

All over the world, news agencies are reporting in everyone's living room, about the, "We Are the World" type atmosphere, buzzing the world media. A simulcast of seven different space mission controls centers. Starting with…

- 1. NASA's Mission Control Center,
- 2. Beijing Aerospace Command and Control Center.
- 3. RKA Mission Control Center of the Russian Federal Space Agency in Korolyo Russia.
- 4. Mobile Servicing System Control and Training at Saint-Hubert, Quebec.
- 5 the Columbus Control Center (Col-CC) at the German Aerospace Center in Oberpfaffenhofen Germany.
- 6. The ATV Control Centre (ATV-CC) at the Toulouse Space Centre (CST) in Toulouse, France.

- 7. Tsukuba Space Center (TKSC) in Tsukuba, Japan

They will be briefing the world, and fielding questions of the historic twelve-person spacewalk, that has been planned for about two years now. Let's break away to April Powers, of WPVO News in Philadelphia.

"We are stationed outside N.A.S.A. Mission Control Center, here at the Lyndon B. Johnson Space Center, in Houston Texas. The MCC also manages the U.S. portions of the International Space Station, (ISS). We are here to report the long awaited multinational twelve astronaut spacewalk, which will take place in three days."

"In a few minutes, we will be going live with a question and answer session with the one and only, Dr. Edward Blast Jr.

Dr. Blast is a lifelong mission control leader, that put Houston and the mission center, in the history books with famous quotes like, "The Eagle has rested".

"Also, he is the person the Mission Control Center is dedicated to. With Dr. Blast, there will be other mission control leaders in the session."

"Let's now listen in, to the introduction of Dr. Blast, and his valuable insight on the upcoming mission."

Everyone will look to their television screens, and monitors around the world, as these mission control leaders speak. The mission will be simulcast around the world in 126 languages.

"Good evening, all you great citizens around the world. My name is Dr. Edward Blast Jr. Thank you in advance for the opportunity to speak on behalf of the newly improved International Space Agency. A unified space travel agency that will break all cultural, race, religion, and national barriers in the name of space travel."

"I am happy to be announcing three historic events unfolding in this year of 2020."

"The first event will be the unveiling, and cutting of the ribbon, of the newly renovated International Space Station."

"The new Space Station is triple the size it was in 2010, when it could only hold six astronaut crew members at a time."

"The newly renovated Space Station can house a crew of twenty now. It has a newly built runway landing strip built into its extension, so space vehicles can fly in and fly out, without and special docking procedures. The second of the two great announcements I have, is the unveiling of the new N.A.S.A. spacecraft called, "The Genesis One Space Cruiser."

After nine long years since the last Shuttle mission was retired, we put a program in place for the private sector to compete, to develop the new up to date space flying craft. The Genesis One Space Cruiser was the winning space vehicle built by, Morehead Spartan Space Aeronautics Inc."

"Now with the new I.S.S., and the new Space Cruiser, there's one more surprise we would like to reveal."

"We have five American astronauts along with two European, one French, one Canadian, one Japanese, one Russian, and one Chinese cosmonaut. They are all getting together on one mission, for a unified spacewalk. This spacewalk mission of twelve astronauts between these great nations, will be blasting off from locations around the world."

"Then they will rendezvous and join at the International Space Station. The same location where we have cameras and microphones. Also, video, to simulcast around the world, to see all the astronauts coming out of the I.S.S. one by one and introduced as if they were international soccer stars."

"That is when they will, one by one perform a spacewalk outside the new, and improved International Space Station. Tethered with just a cable as a lifeline from the vast infinity of space."

"Then once all twelve astronauts, or cosmonauts if you prefer, are all out, they will join hands in a straight line."

"Why are they doing this you may ask? Well, these past years we have all been working together at the new and improved I.S.S. We have been working in perfect harmony, as we look down at the Earth, and watch news feeds of how our nations, and countries cannot see eye to eye. Even worse, it seems people in each country cannot agree how their own country should run."

"There are religions fighting with religions. There is still racism spreading like a cancer in the world. Then you take space exploration, and all those barriers are broken through. Space is the only place, outside of the Earth, where there is peace."

"What better place can we show our leaders and nations how to lead, than the newly improved International Space Station?"

"These twelve astronauts will be joined together hand in hand, spread out in space for as long as it takes to get their leaders to recognize Space travel, as a new frontier of world peace."

"They can eventually meet at the I.S.S, and look down at our great blue planet, and maybe from up here, they can see how small their problems really are. We want to start manned space flights of world leaders to the I.S.S. for meetings, and summits between them. We believe from this station they will see it doesn't matter what color you are, or what faith you belong, to be able to work together."

"Life is too precious, to be waving arms against each other. What we are trying to accomplish is world peace, more funding for space travel, and exploration from the public masses, also governments."

"Let me explain how we chose our astronauts here in the United States. Out of three hundred qualified candidates, we wanted to have a diverse crew of different faiths, race, and backgrounds. We wanted all military personnel in this joint venture."

"For it will take severe endurance, like the endurance-trained in the military branches, to pull off this mission."

"The other countries were to follow the same picking, with as many diverse, religious background qualified astronauts. At this time, I will take on questions from the media on details of this mission. Ok you, young man, you can be the first to question."

"Hello, my name is Rick Gaunt, from W.H.Y.T. in Houston. I would like to know how long this mission will take? "

"Well, our lift off will be seventy-two hours and counting down. That is contingent on whether all the space vehicles from all locations will have the weather clearance, and no maintenance issues."

"This sounds like an easy mission, just throw astronauts up in space, and let them hold hands until the cows come home. It is so complicated, getting all these space vehicles to do this at one time. It is a shot in the dark that it will go on the first try."

"Once we do have clearance it should take about a day to get all the astronauts safely aboard the I.S.S., then the briefings and preparation for the actual spacewalk should take another day."

"If everything goes like clockwork, they could dangle hand in hand for days on out. Of course, the human chain will be rotating for personal meals, breaks and daily prayer. We need to keep them protected from flying space debris, and solar radiation. I will take the next question. You young lady in the red dress."

"Hello, my name is Sara Silvers from W.J.D.R. in Memphis, and I would like to know, in a world that needs to be politically correct, and not discriminate. How does N.A.S.A. seem to pull this off without backlash?"

"Well, the only answer I have, is you can never make everyone happy all the time. Because of diverse divide in this world, we sorted out, and I'm sure our counter parting Space agencies followed us in picking the best qualified people for the mission, while seeking as many beliefs, and backgrounds those parameters would allow us."

"The men and women in our selection process did a very good job picking our final candidates. Next question please, the young lady over there."

"Hello, my name is April Powers of W.P.V.O. News in Philadelphia. Dr., you mentioned your final candidates, can you elaborate on these five astronauts, and where they originate?" "Good question, Ms. Powers. Why yes, I have clearance to brief you on our five wonderful candidates."

"Let me start out by saying, all of our candidates are American born citizens, and are in all ranks of our fine military."

"Let's start with U.S.N. Lieutenant Mission Specialist, Eve S. McGovern. Eve is an International Mission Specialist from Trenton N.J."

"Next, we have U.S.A.F. Colonel, Malone L. Akbar. He is an International Mission Specialist. He is from Spokane Washington."

"Next is U.S.A.F. Lieutenant Colonel, Jeremiah D Edelman. He is a N.A.S.A., Flight Engineer. Jeremiah is from San Diego California."

"Next, we have U.S.N. Lieutenant Commander, Maurice J Kālu. Maurice is from Honolulu Hawaii."

Finally, there is U.S.A.F. Captain Adam C. Pinkert. Adam is from Houston Texas."

"Adam is a mission specialist with seven flown shuttle missions under his belt. There you are folks, our final selection of astronauts, qualified to take this mission on. They are all in day seven of a ten-day mandatory quarantine, so they won't be available for comment until they are out, and that will be the day of our planned Space Cruiser takeoff."

"Ok, I will take one more question, and then I have to finalize this meeting. I hope I was very helpful in describing N.A.S.A.'s current space mission. You, young man, your turn now."

"Hello, my name is David Freidman of W.T.Y.P. in Wichita Kansas. I have just one question. What is this mission being called?"

Dr. Edward. Blast Jr. looked at the young reporter with authority and said, mission "Space Walk for Peace."

All the reporters were taking notes and shuffling around as the Dr. exited the stage.

They were all turning on their surround lighting to do their live news interviews with their corresponding cities. For three days the world started preparations for mission "Space Walk for Peace." It became a phenomenon across the country, and the world.

Events were held, and people were wearing tee-shirts with the "Space Walk for Peace" logo on it. It was media frenzy, with all the countries around the world talking about the same thing, wondering if this event can bring change and peace to their country.

A multinational space force leading the way for world peace, was a new concept that no one has heard of, and made many people jump on board to the idea.

Still with the world leaders already interviewed, it seems they had a wait and see attitude. This news was nothing new, but this spacewalk was sure a big thing. The stage was set for this historic event, as the final day approached.

The meteorologist was keeping track of the weather and keeping in touch of the other countries weather patterns.

It was dicey from day to day, with the Jet Stream bringing clouds, and precipitation to the eastern countries, and disturbances coming out of the Gulf. The international Space Station was getting ready to accept the space vehicles, dockings in series. A feat never attempted, with seven space vehicles from eight different countries, and the payload associated with it.

There were satellites stationed by multiple news stations around the world all focused on the Space Station. There was a slew of media at the Houston Space Center.

The preparations were immense as peace protest broke out in every city around the world leading up to launch day. There were a lot of concerns for the safety of the astronauts in the harsh environment of an extended spacewalk.

State leaders joined along, and the whole world was getting anxious, and very excited for this big event. Once the technology of The Space Cruiser news has been let out of the bag, most other countries followed.

They scrapped their current space program launching devices, to the new modern take off like an airplane, and fly into space maneuver.

So, the new cruiser design was born all around the world. It was much less expensive and can make a round trip journey to the I.S.S. in just about half the fuel and time, than the conventional shuttle vehicles. It was an easy sell to the Europeans.

It expanded space travel around the world to more countries, and exposed space travel to a bigger audience. It was just a few years ago, when Russia had the only means to fly cosmonauts to the I.S.S., and other countries, as America paid them millions to take their astronauts to the I.S.S.

It was a dark age in space travel, while all along N.A.S.A. was quietly putting together a new space program to lead the rest of the world in space travel.

"The Reunion"

Adam steps through the old beach house front door. "What do you call a scary chicken?" He asks the waiting crew inside the conference room.

Maurice replies, "What is that Adam?"

Eve Replies, "Is that the first thing you ask after not seeing us for ten days Adam?"

Adam replies, "A poultry Geist Maurice," He said with a slur.

"And for you Eve, what am I supposed to say, after being all "cooped up" for ten days?" "Buck! Buck!" He said, while he flapped his arms like a chicken.

Jeremiah laughed out loud, as everyone joined him at laughing at Adam's response.

The old beach house was a favorite place for all astronauts to relax, with the crew or family the day before the launch.

The beach house is the property of N.A.S.A. about a mile from old Launch Pad Forty, and a new runway.

The old Space Shuttle landing strip is for the new "Genesis One" at the John F. Kennedy Space Center in Florida.

"Dam, check this joint out, this is badass," says Adam.

"Yea we were scoping this place before you arrived. It's pretty cool here," said Jeremiah.

Malone said, "There were a lot of famous astronauts here before us, this is something special man."

Adam questioned, "How do you know that Malone?"

Before he could answer, Eve spoke up and said, "Their freaking signatures are on the wine bottles on the fireplace mantle."

Adam walks over to the mantle looks and says, "Daaaaam!" "Yea if these walls could talk," said Maurice.

Adam replied, "You probably couldn't hear them because of the sound of all these seagulls."

Jeremiah added, "They converted this joint into conference rooms after they scrapped the shuttle missions in 2011."

Adam walks over to the patio doors, opens them, walks out on a giant wooden deck, then walks to the middle, and yells at the top of his lungs, "Houston can you hear me!"

Maurice looks a Malone and Jeremiah, and gestures with a smile, "Keep an eye on this guy." They just laughed.

Malone stands up and says, "I am getting my swimsuit on, and headed straight out to that ocean, and hitting the waves if anyone wants to join?"

"That is a freaking great idea", said Eve. "I want to."

Maurice said, "I'll hang back to cook some breakfast on the grill, while you guys work up early morning appetites."

Adam replies, "Sounds like a plan from my main man," as he heads out to the beach with the other three crew members.

Maurice heads back to the kitchen and puts another pot of coffee on. Then he looks in the refrigerator, for some bacon to throw on the grill. He opens the door to find the refrigerator stocked with everything under the sun. Maurice thinks to himself, "Well, well, we are going to eat good today." He reaches in, and pulls out a bag of hash browns, a pound of bacon, and a dozen eggs. His stomach grumbles, and he says, "I am starving."

Eve walking through the sand, as the sea breeze blows back her shoulder length hair. "Oh my, she says." What a beautiful day out here by the water."

Jeremiah replies, "Yes indeed the weather is just right for a ride into space tomorrow."

Eve responds. "Let's not think about that and enjoy our last day here."

Malone says, "What on Earth do you mean by that Eve?"

Eve said, "Well you just can't take our mission for granted, we all remember Challenger. You just have to enjoy every minute you are here. One minute you are here, and the next minute you are gone."

Malone replies, "I can feel you sister, we all have that thought in the back of our minds. But for some of us thought or fear is the driving force behind us to move this nation forward. I think we learn from our mistakes to better our future. I really believe that."

Adam says, "Isn't this the shit."

Jeremiah says, "What do you see Adam?"

Adam replies, "We are standing here today on the beach watching the sand fade to the water, and the water fades to the sky.

Tomorrow we will look from the sky, we will watch the water fade to the beach, talk about extremes!"

Malone says to Adam, "What are you a freaking philosopher now?" Then he wrestles Adam down to the sand.

While all that was happening, Eve made it to the waves. "The water is warm guys, come in and play."

Adam brushes the sand off and yells, "Last one in don't get to kiss the mermaid." The three men joined the water, and the four were spending a late morning doing what every astronaut did in the past, these astronauts were following right in their footsteps. After some time, all the astronauts emerge from the waves, and grab their towels to head back to the beach house.

Eve runs up the beach house steps and says, "I have the first shower."

Then Adam said, "Well if you knew anything about a beach house you would know there is an outside shower like this one over here, so that makes me first."

Malone said, walking up the beach house steps, "I will just drip dry and go for that delicious smelling brunch that Maurice is cooking up."

Jeremiah said, "I am with Malone, I rather be a dirty bird with a full belly." So the two go out to the patio area where Maurice is, and see the spread he has set out on the table.

Jeremiah says, "Now that is what I call a spread Malone!"

Malone says, "Yea man, that's some good cooking's."

Maurice replied, "Now sit down and enjoy my friends." The three sat at the table, and then Eve and Adam join the feast.

After brunch all but Maurice is helping to clean up the meal. Maurice cooked it, so he was excused by a vote, and retired to the conference room where the flat screen T.V. is.

Maurice turned the T.V. on, and right away coverage was on the news of the five astronauts.

Maurice yells to the crew, "Hey look we're famous."

The rest of the crew made their way into the conference room to see what was going on. On the T.V. the commentator started with, "Now introducing Ms. April Powers of W.P.V.O. News in Philadelphia. We have live coverage of the upcoming international space mission set to take off tomorrow."

"While we wait for that to happen, let's look into who our five heroes are. Let's take a different spin on their professions like U.S.N. Lieutenant, Mission Specialist, and Commander, which are some of their titles, and bring the astronauts down to Earth, and make some Earthly references to them."

"The first of our astronauts is a young lady named, Eve S. McGovern. Eve is a local Christian girl from over the river in Trenton N.J. So that makes Eve our, "Jersey Girl.""

"Then we have a young man named Adam C. Pinkert, and Adam is from Houston Texas, so let's refer to Adam as our, "Cowboy.""

"Next we have a young man named Malone L. Akbar. Malone is from Spokane Washington."

"So that gives Malone our nickname, "The Chief.""

"Next, we have another young man, and his name is Jeremiah D Edelman, and Mr. Edelman is from San Diego California, so let's call Jeremiah, 'The Surfer.""

"Now at last but not least, is one more young man named Maurice J Kālu, now Mr. Kālu is from Honolulu Hawaii. So, let's refer to Mr. Kālu as, "The Islander.""

"So, let's review our five Hero's, now they have their Philadelphia nicknames as, Jersey Girl, The Cowboy, The Chief, The Surfer and The Islander."

"Stay tuned at six, we will review the other seven foreign astronauts, and cosmonauts that will join our five on this international mission, "Space Walk for Peace.""

As the news clip ended, the five astronauts looked around the conference table, and looked at each other.

There was silence for about five seconds, then all laughter broke out. They were just pointing fingers at each other in that conference room, and laughing their asses off, at the nickname reporter April Powers gave them. Adam was first to catch his breath.

He looked at Maurice and said, "I do not have to call you Maurice anymore, Mr. Island Boy!"

Maurice replied, "You got it Cowboy."

Eve then said, "I am pretty cool with Jersey girl, what do you think Island Boy?"

Then they all laughed again until Maurice caught his breath and said, "As long as you do not call me the Surfer."

That just started the laughing again. Jeremiah said, "I hope they do not give me that name for my handle call on the space mission."

Eve replied, "You know, that reporter from Philly has some spunk, you go girl."

Maurice then said, "let's not forget to tune in at six, and watch the coverage on the other seven astronauts, after all, I happened to doze off at the briefing when the commander was giving us the info on these guys."

Adam looked at Eve and said in his "John Wayne" impersonation, "Hey Jersey Gal, ye ever dream you'd take a ride in space with eleven guys?"

Eve returned with pointing to Adams crotch saying, "You know with one of them, you can hope, pray, or wish to get one of these, pointing to her crotch.

However, with one of these I can get eleven of them Cowboy."

The other three crew members at one time said, "Oooooooh hooooooooooooo, I guess she told you Cowboy." Then they all laughed again.

"Ok, that is enough, now it's time for reading", said Eve, as she retired to the den for some quiet time. Maurice said to the guys," There is an awesome ping pong table in the lower level. Is anyone game?"

Jeremiah replied, "I am in." The same time Malone said the same thing, "I am in." Then Malone said, "Well, I'll watch and play the winner."

Maurice said to Adam, "What about you cowboy?"

Adam replied, "I'll pass, there's a good matinee on T.V., I'll just hang here, put my feet up and watch. Maybe I'll catch an afternoon cat nap if it gets boring."

"Ok," said Maurice, as the three headed downstairs. While the five astronauts are being occupied in the beach house, we will zoom out of the beach house.

We will travel a mile down the road to the John F. Kennedy Space Center, to the old Launch Pad Forty where the new "Genesis One' spacecraft is being stored. It is in the hanger by the new runway for the Space Cruiser, as N.A.S.A. is making last minute tweaks to the Space Cruiser.

As we go inside, the Space cruiser looks like something out of a science fiction movie. It resembles a small fighter jet except all the edges are rolled and curved as the wings are also bent upwards at the tips.

The crew is working feverishly on the craft, checking and double checking the life support systems, the electronics, all the controls, the fuel, and the list goes on and on.

The media caravan is outside the Space Center setting up one of the most news covered events in Kennedy Space Center history.

Because of the ending of one era with the Space Shuttle missions, and starting a new era with N.A.S.A., and Genesis One, the atmosphere around here feels like the old days.

Heading back to the beach house where the five astronauts are.

We see everyone has fallen into an afternoon cat nap. The three young men that exhausted themselves playing ping pong, to Adam falling asleep watching TV, to Eve succumbing to after reading a mystery novel. Well, it is early evening, and Maurice wakes up on the sofa in the lower deck.

He says, "Wake up guys; we still have a whole evening together before our mission in the morning."

Then Jeremiah and Malone come too. "What the heck happened, Maurice asked."

"I think the last night in quarantine kept us all restless waiting for it to end," exclaimed Jeremiah.

Maurice countered with, "You might be on to something there Mr. Surfer."

"It sounds quiet upstairs also so let's go see what's happening up there."

As the three men were coming up the wooden steps from the lower level, the thundering sound from the bare wood steps startled Eve in the den, and she popped up as if she was never asleep.

"Hi guys I was waiting for you to wake up from your naps", she said.

"No, no don't do it, I'll never make it," was the sound the four heard coming from the conference room where Adam was napping.

Eve says, "Looks like Cowboy is talking in his sleep again."

Maurice walks over to Adam and shrugs him on the shoulder and says, "Adam wake up."

Adam startled, comes out of his sleep just fine stating, "what time is it?"

Malone looks at the clock over the mantel and says" its 5:00pm, I am headed up to shower and change for the night."

Jeremiah said, "Yea, I am in as soon as you are out."

Eve looks out onto the deck and sees a barbeque grille and says, "Hey, I do not know how hungry everyone is, so I will just fire up the grill to get it hot."

Maurice says, "Yes there's all kind of good things to throw on the grill for dinner, and it looks like it is going to be a great night to sit out on the deck and talk about tomorrow's mission."

Adam says," sounds like a plan Island Boy." Then Adam laughs and says, "I am going up to put some comfortable clothes on for the night, I'll be back."

So as three crew members get changed, Maurice and Eve start preparation for dinner on the grill.

Maurice looks in the refrigerator and says," There are five nice Angus sirloin steaks in here, and to top it off a couple bottles of red wine cooled in here."

Eve says, "Perfect, I will prepare the sides, and wrap some potatoes in foil to put on the grill."

So, a little time passes as Maurice is flipping steaks on the grille, and eve is setting the large glass top table with matching chairs.

Adam, Malone, and Jeremiah all enter the patio area. Maurice yells, "Sit down boys, and let's have our last supper together."

With a smile, Adam replies, "Hey partner, that's not funny Island Boy." So, the whole crew is settled at the table on the deck on a beautiful August evening as Maurice serves their steak dinners, and Eve walks around and pours the wine.

Jeremiah says, "Hey isn't it time for that news report on the other astronauts?"

Malone says, "Yep, it is that time, it is just about 6:00 now."

Adam says, "Hey how about everyone stays just where they are, as I will open the patio door and go inside to tilt the TV to face us out here. I will grab the remote for the volume." Eve said, "Cowboy that's the best idea you had all day."

Then Adam does his best "John Wayne" voice and said, "Your welcome sister." Then Adam sets the TV up and takes his seat as they all listen in while they are eating.

"Hello, this is Jim Harner, of W.P.V.O. Channel 16 News in Philadelphia. Welcome to the 6:00 broadcast, and the big story tonight is the long-awaited international spacewalk dubbed, "Space Walk for Peace." It is a seven nation plight for world peace, and space advancement. In this segment, we will focus on the seven foreign astronauts, not covered in our reporter April Power's coverage segment at twelve. So, let's go to Ms. April Powers live at John F. Kennedy Space Center in south Florida. "April, are you there?"

"Yes Jim, I am here with the chief executive Colonel Jack K. Sullivan, of "Mission Space Walk for Peace."

" Colonel, how are things shaping up in the final hours of this mission?"

"Hello April and thank you for inquiring.

"We are pleased to let everyone know; we are on schedule with our maiden blast off of the 2020 "Space Walk for Peace." We are in communication with seven other space command centers on the globe, on weather conditions and blastoff schedules."

"Colonel, is weather an important factor in the blast off procedure?"

"Yes, and no April, you see not like conventional lift offs, or like the Space Shuttles lift offs, when you need pristine weather conditions. These Genesis blastoffs are more similar to airline takeoffs."

"Well, the Genesis cruiser can take off in the rain, but once it reaches a certain altitude, where the rocket boosters kick in, it cannot encounter any major wind turbulence. Our counterpart space agencies are using the same type space vehicle."

"Reaching space is not so much an issue, as all seven space cruisers landing on the ISS runway, dropping off its payload, and departing for the next space cruiser to land in a series."

"Colonel, speaking of the other six space cruisers, there are seven astronauts in all, with the European cruiser carrying two. My question, can you give us some insight on theses seven astronauts?"

"Why yes Ms. Powers, let's start off with our Russian counterpart cosmonaut Dmitri S. Federoff. He is a well experienced cosmonaut, with four space station missions under his belt."

"He will be flying in the Russian space cruiser. Then we have our European counterparts with two astronauts.

"A German astronaut named Axel P. Klein, and The English astronaut Mr. Charles G. Jones. They will blast off from Germany."

"Then we have our Japanese counterpart astronaut, Mr. Haruto L. Tanaka. He will blast off from Japan. Next, we have our French counterpart astronaut, Mr. Jacques R. Dubois. He will blast off from France"

"Next, we have our Canadian counterpart astronaut, Alexandre H. Roy, and finally our Chinese Counterpart Zhang K. Chen. He will blast off from Beijing China."

"Well, that is quite a list Colonel, plus our five wonderful astronauts. I can see what a feat this is going to be tomorrow, not only having a maiden flight of one of our own spacecrafts, but maiden flights for others also. "Thank you, Colonel Sullivan for the information." "Well, people you heard it here first. So, I hope our astronauts get to bed early tonight, because they have one hell of a day tomorrow."

"One note from Colonel Sullivan, is that none of the twelve astronauts will be flying their space cruisers. They will all have personal pilots to drop them off, then return the space cruisers."

"Signing off, this is reporter April Powers WPVO Channel 16 News, from the John F. Kennedy Space Center, Merritt Island, Brevard County in Florida."

"Thank you, April, now we will go to other news........."

"Ok, looks like we will have to review our briefing papers on the other astronauts," said Eve.

"Well, we will all be holding hands tomorrow morning, so we will have plenty of time to get to know them," said Malone.

"This steak is delicious," said Adam.

"Yea, it is such a great meal," said Jeremiah. "Can you pass the wine?"

"Easy on that wine," said Eve. "You do not need a hangover, traveling G-force speeds on our climb to the stars tomorrow."

Jeremiah replied, "I hear you "Jersey Girl.""

How long do you guys think we will be out there on the spacewalk?"

"I think until most of the Superpower leaders acknowledge our plight," said Adam.

"I think the public pressure will be the determining factor," said Malone.

"How is that, "Surfer Man.?" How can the public pressure governments that don't listen to them?" asked Maurice.

"Well, when I say the public, I also include the media, the actual people of the public that makes the officials who they are. The media can make or break a politician."

"Point well made," said Maurice.

"Well let's take the few hours we have left together to relax, and enjoy the summer ocean breeze," said Jeremiah. As soon as he said that, the Cape House phone rang.

Adam rose and walked inside to answer the phone. Eve pointed to Maurice to grab the remote to turn the TV down, so they can hear Adam talking. "Yea, ok, yea ok, what do you mean the mission is cancelled?"

The rest of the crew dropped their jaws and eyeballs wide open, as Adam walked slowly back from the phone with his head down.

"What did they say, asked Maurice?"

Adam slowly raised his head and said, "That was Mission Control, they told us to call our loved ones, and a limo will be here at 5:30AM sharp, to pick us up."

Then there was a silence, Eve yelled "And what?"

Adam with his devil looking face replied, "to take us to Launch Pad Forty, for our flight tomorrow." There was a big sigh of relief from the crew.

"You're always playing with our heads Cowboy," said Jeremiah. "You jerk," exclaimed Eve. Maurice and Malone were laughing with relief.

"Let's all have a final toast to a wonderful relationship with this crew, as we need to pull together, and make sure we get back alive. All for one and one for all," said Adam.

So, all five crew members raised their glasses in unison, and all at once said, Cheers!

"So, what is the order of the walk Maurice? You being the Commander, I figured they gave you that information," said Jeremiah.

"Yes indeed," Maurice said, "the Americans will lead the spacewalk, so that means we will be blasting off first."

"We will land at the I.S.S. first, and we will also be introduced to the public first. We will lead the twelve-person line in the space walk."

"What a special honor, to be the first crew flying in a new generation spacecraft for N.A.S.A. and leading the way for world peace and space exploration," Said Eve.

"They will be announcing our names, as we walk out that door, for the entire world to see. I am going to feel like a rock star, for one moment in time," Said Adam.

"You can ask any rock star Adam, and I'll bet you they would love to be in your shoes," said Maurice.

"Why would you say that "Island Man?" Adam asked.

"I say that because they can make any music hit, and maybe there is a very tiny chance that their hit will make it where our mission will. That my friend, is one for the books, because we are making history."

"A point very well-made Maurice," Malone replied. "We are about to undertake a mission that no other astronaut has ever done. We could ultimately be on a longer spacewalk than any other astronaut before us."

"Well, I am tired of talking about this. We all better get to our cell phones, and call our loved ones, and tell them how much we love them," said Jeremiah.

So, all five astronauts retired to different rooms in the Cape house, and dialed their phones, calling their families. After that, they all prepared to retire for the night, setting their alarms for 5AM, and charging their cell phones. 5:30AM comes very early and fast, and they all need to be ready for that limo from the Kennedy Space Center just down the road.

"Genesis One"

Brrrrrrrrrrrrrring, brrrrrrrrrring, brrrrrrrrrrrrrrring, brrrrrrrrrrrrrrrrrrg, brrrrrrrrrrrrrrrrring!

5:00AM and the weathers fine.

"I have the first shower, you all get in line," says Adam, as he reaches over to slap the alarm. He hops from the bed, stretches and lets out a big yawn. The other three men are rustling to get another minute sleep. He exits the sleeping quarters, and walks down the hall, and notices a familiar aroma coming from downstairs.

"Is that you Adam?" A voice comes from below.

"Yepper, "Jersey Girl," Adam replies in his "John Wayne" voice. "Save me a cup of Joe cowgirl, while I wrestle up a hot shower."

Eve replies, "Sure thing "Cowboy," as the rest of the crew gets up and ready.

It's 5:30am, and all the crew members are sitting out on the front deck porch, waiting for their Limo to show up. "Is everyone ready?" Maurice asks. The rest reply "All ready to go," a rehearsed saying practiced by astronauts. Its 5:35am, the limo rolls up, and the driver gets out to opens all the doors. The crew enters the limo. The limo drives up the road, as Eve turns and looks at the Cape House, fading in the distance.

"Well, its T-minus sixty minutes to blastoff," exclaimed Jeremiah.

"Yea this one is going to be great, I do not have to pilot this mission," said Maurice.

Malone said, "Bring it on man; I cannot wait for the rush."

Adam said in his 'John Wayne" voice, "I cannot wait to lasso this gal pilgrim," referring to the Genesis Space Cruiser nicknamed "Marilyn."

Meanwhile at Kennedy Space Center, there are hundreds of news media cameras, and reporters sitting there waiting for the limo to drive by the Visitor's Center parking lot, as it heads to Headquarters, Operations and Checkout.

As the limo passes the Astronauts Hall of Fame on the SR 405, the N.A.S.A. causeway, the crew can see the buildup of media on their right. Once the crew is briefed, and dressed in their Base Suits, there will be a fifteen-minute media picture and interview session. That is when they will be whisked down the road to checkout, and then shuttled to the runway where the "Genesis One" Space Craft is waiting.

The Presidential looking Lincoln goes rolling by the Visitors Center, with camera's flashing like a concert strobe light show.

The limo pulls up to the guarded operations and checkout building. The driver gets out and opens the door while the "Fab Five", walk out like it was the

Beatles revolution all over again. They walk into the doors of the Operation Building.

They walk down a long white hallway, straight to a N.A.S.A. conference room. They all grab a chair and wait for a   briefing. Just then Colonel Jack K. Sullivan walks up to the podium.

"Hello Hero's, you wonder why I call you heroes. The fact of the matter is, this whole mission is a shot in the dark. There are so many things that can go wrong. We can have another tragedy here on our hands, and just in case you do not make it back from this mission, I am giving you your badges, and rankings of hero's now. Do I make myself clear?"

"Yes sir," said the crew in unison, Maurice gestured to the Colonel,

Colonel Sullivan said, "Go ahead Commander."

Maurice asked the Colonel, "What kind of dangers are we facing here?"

"Well to start we never flew six astronauts in a Space Cruiser. It's a much longer trip into space than a rocket, because of the trajectory of the flight.

We don't know if the structure will fail during a long G force travel time. We did plenty of tests that say it's worthy, but no actual real flights. Then we have a correlation of seven Space Cruisers, from all parts of the world meeting up, and landing like an airline style runway in space.

Then you will dangle by a tether cable, on the longest spacewalk known to man. They should have tested monkeys before you guys, for God's sake."

"Boy you really know how to make a girl feel welcomed," exclaimed Eve.

"The number one reason we picked you for this mission Lieutenant, is that your female, and we need you to keep this crew inline when the shit hits the fan, because we know your resolve, and leadership under difficult pressure situations. Do you feel welcomed now sweetheart?"

Adam raised his hand, and the Colonel nodded at him to speak.

"Don't you think you're a little harsh on us Colonel?"

"Harsh," "Well, listen here, and listen good. I am the only voice you are going to hear on this mission from this planet. I am your control, and you are my Major Tom. You need to listen to everything I say to stay alive. So, go out there and see the media, and sign autographs, but once you're in that Space Cruiser, I am suddenly going to be your best friend."

"When all those bells and whistles, and blinking red lights go off in that tin can you're flying, I will be your lifeline. Do I clarify myself?"

"Yes sir," said Adam.

"Before I continue, does anyone else have a question?" Colonel Sullivan asked with his determined stern voice. There was silence. "Ok, now let's go over everything that will happen until blast off. Once you're in the cruiser, that will be the next time you hear from me."

"Next you will go to the showers that will wash any bacteria off your bodies, because bacteria thrive in a space environment. Also, if you didn't shower this morning, I don't think you'll want to smell yourself, while you're in your space suits during the walk."

"Once you all are showered, you will be given your space jumpsuits to wear as under clothing for your main space suits. We call them civilian suits. They are all nice and pretty, with the N.A.S.A. space cruiser symbol, and American flag patch."

"Perfect dressing for the cameras, you will have fifteen minutes with cameras and microphones in your face. This will be history in the making."

"Then a transporter will take you to the runway, where you will finish dressing into your space suits at the transport center, then climb aboard where the "Genesis One' Space Cruiser is waiting. You will meet your chauffeur, Pilot Lieutenant, Samuel Walker."

"You can call him Sammy, he won't mind. Commander Kālu, you will be the co-pilot on this mission, just as you trained to be. Then there will be the conventional countdown, and then the take off. That is when you will hear my sweet voice again."

"Ok, this briefing is over. Good luck crew, all the eyes of the world will be upon you from this moment on." Then the Colonel turned right and exited the room. "Whew, what the hell did we get into here," asked Jeremiah?

"Just relax, everything will run smooth, I can feel it. They are just trying to see if we get rattled," said Eve. "Do you really think this mission will go array with all the money, and reputation of this space programs future on the line? I think not."

Malone added "I'm going to have a lot of confidence in Colonel Sullivan, because the first thing he said about you being our rock Eve, is already coming true."

"Awe, you're so sweet "Surfer Man" Thank you," said Eve. "OK, let's go shower then meet the press."

The crew left to get ready for flight, as the crew was getting ready, the media could enter the checkout area on the outside grounds.

This event is grabbing so much worldwide media attention, you can compare this to the biggest sporting event in history, and then ten times that, that's how big this is.

There's this underlying feeling in the world right now with all the tensions between countries, and all the military posturing that the world is longing for world peace and looking for someone or some event to lead the way for everyone.

Now the world media is opening the door for this space event, to break the ice in world peace negotiations. The space crew comes out from the doors donned in their pearly white space jumpsuits.

The cameras are flashing like a strobe, as each of the crew is separated by media, for individual interviews.

Reporter; "Astronaut Eve, do you realize what you are about to do, and what it means for mankind?"

Eve; "Yes I do, and I am damn proud of it. Where else can a Girl from Trenton New Jersey sit on the world stage, and represent the general feelings of the entire world?"

Reporter; "Astronaut Maurice, what will it be like, to co-pilot the newest space vehicle in the world?"

Maurice; "I have been trained by the best aviation teachers on this planet. I am proud to be an airman, and an astronaut. It reminds me of when I was a kid, and the newest astronaut spacesuit was in the store window for my GI Joe doll, and we could not afford to buy it."

"I remember pushing my nose up to the glass window and wishing my G.I. Joe could be wearing it. I would never dream so big, to actually become that G.I. Joe, wearing that space suit, getting ready to co-pilot the latest space machine."

Reporter to astronaut Jeremiah; "If you could say one word to all the leaders of the world while doing the spacewalk, what could we be reading your lips saying?"

Jeremiah; "Well, that word would simply be "One."

Reporter; "What would you mean by the word?"

Jeremiah: "One world, one belief, one law, one truth, one society, one love, one peace."

Reporter: "Malone, if you had one word to say while doing the walk, what would your word be?"

Malone: "I will be with my brothers from every faith, color, and creed, and the word that comes to my mind is No! No more war, no more bloodshed, no more starvation, no more hate, no violence, no more tears."

Reporter: "Adam you are last to be interviewed.

Can you describe what the world feeling will be while you and your crew, and all the astronauts from all parts of this world that are about to take this historic spacewalk, while you put your lives on the line for world peace?"

Adam, "I really think this mission is historical just by its nature of flying the maiden voyage of the "Genesis One", also coming together with other people from other countries to break the new frontier of peace, and by going out of this world to do it."

"I think the world feeling will be, well if these people would go to such lengths to stand united for peace thousands of miles above us. Then I think I can turn to that neighbor that I see every day but never acknowledge they're alive, and we all have one."

"I think I will say hello to them tomorrow when they come out to get the paper."

Just as Adam was finished speaking a voice came over the loudspeaker.

"Attention Please!" then a pause. "Media session is about to conclude. Our astronauts are about to be escorted to their destination. We ask that all media personnel, please stand back and "watch the tram car please."

Then the white transport car pulled up, and the five astronauts entered the car. That didn't stop the media from putting on their giant strobe light show, as cameras were flashing every direction filming the transport car driving up the runway. The car stops at the transport station for the astronauts to dress into their space suits.

A few minutes later the astronauts come walking out of the transport station dressed in full space suits, holding their space helmets, walking in a straight line to the runway, where Pilot Lieutenant Samuel Walker is waiting to greet the crew. As the crew pulls up to the aircraft, Lieutenant Walker stands erect with a salute, then all the crew follows with a salute.

Pilot Walker says, "At ease, how do you like those suits?" the Lieutenant asked.

Adam answered "I never seen a suit like this one. You get into it and then find out you can live in it. You can sleep, eat, drink and breath in it, and all body fluids and bad breath are immediately extracted from you, and quarantined in the back-calf compartment on your legs." "Hey Jersey girl, you won't need to know where the lady's room is. "Eve replies, "TMI Adam."

There they all stand, decked in the latest technology spacesuit. Standing at the latest technological space marvel flying machine, on a bright sunny morning, on a runway in Florida. It's the last time their feet will touch Earth, for who knows how long.

Just then Jeremiah bends down to his knees and kisses the warming asphalt, saying, "Goodbye cruel world, we will return to a new one." Then the pilot opens the passenger doors in the rear. Adam and Malone get into one side, and Eve and Jeremiah climb into the other side rear compartment.

Maurice walks around the rear of the aircraft to the passenger side front compartment, as the pilot gets in the driver's side.

"Check out this ride," said Adam. "All the comforts of the latest luxury limousine cramped into a roomy six passenger pod."

The astronauts are getting familiar with their seating, and Maurice is getting familiar with the flight deck dashboard controls.

There is the voice of Pilot Walker over the cabin intercom, "Welcome and good morning crew, sit back and get comfortable, and look around at the different option controls around you."

"There is the dome dimming control in black on your right, if the sunlight gets too bright on the flight. Then there's the seat adjustment joystick in yellow, to rotate your seat up, down, and turn to the left or right. Once the G force sets in you will not be able to turn your head, and that joystick will come in handy."

"Tucked down between everyone's legs is an emergency pilot controller."

"This will be available to all passengers in case the pilot and co-pilot become incapacitated for some odd reason."

"The aircraft will recognize a non-human control, and automatically engage your controllers to pop up, and a coordinate screen to appear also."

"This will engage on an emergency basis and put the aircraft in autopilot until one of you grabs the controls."

"The last control available is a ripcord pull above your right shoulder. This is for complete ejection from the spacecraft, weather in space or our atmosphere. Each astronaut has one, and I truly hope no one has to pull it. So now that you have yourselves strapped in, and your knowledge of controls, there's one more thing I have to inform you on."

"As you all know this is a spacecraft, and it looks like a military glider, well it's a little of both."

"Let me explain, we will be waiting for the countdown that you will hear in your helmets. Then we will take off down the runway like an airplane."

"We will fly about one thousand miles on a gradual accent going faster, and faster until you feel the rocket boosters kick in. Then we will be in Mach one, then Mach two, then Mach three, G=force speed until the blue-sky turns black."

"The Space Cruiser will rotate one hundred eighty degrees, and our interior capsule will gyro rotate, to stay right side up until we break the atmosphere edge. The space cruiser will right itself once in space."

"Sounds like a rollercoaster maneuver," said Adam.

Pilot: "There is Dramamine in your helmets you can take it if your stomach gets upset."

Jeremiah spoke up and said, "I already took it just listening to your description of the flight."

"Roger that," said the pilot.

Then Mission control came live in everyone's helmet.

Mission control to Pilot; "Are you ready for takeoff?"

Pilot: "Ready!"

Mission control to crew, "Are you ready for takeoff?"

Crew, "Ready!"

Mission,Control:"T-minus 60,59,58,57,56,55,54,53,52,51,50,49,48,47,46,45,44,43,42,41,40,39,38,37,36,35,34,33,32,31,30,29,28,27,26,25,24,23,22,21,20,19,18,17,16,15,14,13,12,11,10,09,08,07,06,05,04,03,02,01,

"TAKE OFF!"

Genesis One fires its rocket jets, and starts down the runway. The band on the ground plays the Star-Spangled Banner, as the Space Cruiser's wheels lifts off the runway. There are two white plumes of smoke trailing the Space Cruiser, as it is fully off the runway, and headed straight out over the ocean off of South Florida.

Meanwhile, every TV station has an emergency interruption in their daily programming all over America, and all over the world showing video, and reporting of all the Space Cruisers, from all around the world taking off in their respective countries.

"It is a world historic event on this day of August 15th in the year Twenty-Twenty," says a World newscaster.

"Here are live clips of the seven Space Cruisers taking off at mission control sights in seven different countries.

"It's a time for the world to celebrate the efforts of these brave astronauts risking their lives, for a mission that's designed to generate world peace. "Let's just take a moment and watch as these magical space machines disappear from the blue sky and enter space.

Back to Genesis One, as the space cruiser lifts into the atmosphere, Eve looks to the left out her window, and says to herself, "goodbye New Jersey, I will be back soon."

The space cruiser is lifting higher, and faster as it goes over the Earth's horizon.

All crew members are alerted to airlock their helmets on and turn on their oxygen.

The ship is entering Mach one speeds, and the G force is felt a little, limiting the crew to move freely.

Maurice announces over the intercom "Get ready crew, we are about to reach hyper speed, so strap in and enjoy the ride."

Just then the awaited announcement came over the helmet speaker. "Good morning Space Crew, this is the crew at mission control."

"We have you at one hundred miles, traveling in Mach one, how are you feeling?"

Pilot to mission control: "The crew is holding fast and steady, as we get ready to engage the rocket boosters.

Pilot: "Permission to engage."

Mission Control: "Permission granted." Pilot Walker flips a switch then all seats tilt back fifteen degrees. Then Pilot Walker presses two red buttons, and two turbo rocket boosters engage. The space cruiser goes from Mach one to Mach two.

The crew can feel the G-force as the Space Cruiser accelerates into the blue sky. Now the crew is gradually lifting into the upper atmosphere. They grab their joysticks and rotate to see each other.

Adam turns to Jeremiah, and puts his thumbs up, while Jeremiah talks into his helmet microphone, "Looking good Cowboy."

Then there was the voice of Colonel Sullivan on the headsets. "I hear some of you are still alive up there, who's the cowboy?"

"That would be Mission specialist Adam Pinkert Colonel," said Maurice.

"Attention all crew members, all replies back will be addressed to Mission Control from here on out," said Colonel Sullivan.

"We are now entering the lower Mesosphere and reaching speeds of Mach three," said the pilot. "Carry on; your ship is on schedule," said Mission Control.

The Genesis One Space Cruiser turns and flips 180 degrees as the inner cabin where the crew is stays upright.

"Whoooah," says Eve.

"Mission control our ship has turned," said the pilot.

" Yes, right on time, the bottom of you ship is designed to protect you in the solar charged Mesosphere, shielding all charged particles from your space cruiser," replied Mission Control. "Your Cruiser will upright when you leave the Mesosphere and reach the Thermosphere."

Adam said, "This is the best ride to space I ever experienced."

"Yea this is one of the coolest rides I was ever on," said Jeremiah.

The space cruiser is traveling through the charged particles in the Mesosphere, and it looks like it is burning up from the speed friction.

Then after a few minutes pass, the space car uprights and the Genesis One is now cruising in space. They went from a fiery violent turbulence, to a perfect tranquility in a matter of minutes.

They were all looking out the windows of the Space Cruiser, down at the silent Earth. Maurice was the first to speak, "Look at that planet, and to think with all the land and oceans, mankind cannot get along.

"The I.S.S"

Jeremiah replied with, "That is what our mission is all about, to get the world to see what we are looking at from up here, to see how small their problems really are.

"That was such a violent event with sparks flying all around the spacecraft, and then all at once there was serenity and everything was smooth sailing, simply amazing," said Adam.

Then the pilot called Mission Control.

"Genesis One to Mission Control, we finally reached the heavens."

Colonel Sullivan from Mission Control replied, "That all depends on what faith you are, Mission Specialist Pinkert." "With a name like mine there's no mistake partner," Adam said to mission control.

The Colonel replies, "Ok in all seriousness crew, you will make one rotation over the Earth until you go over the South Pole.

"For all you who don't know, it's the pole with the most volume of ice. You will see the International Space Station. Your cruiser will be the first to land on the I.S.S. runway."

"When you come to a stop, and exit the Space Cruiser, there will be the cable line with a tether wire there, to hook to your space suit. Then you can pull yourselves to the back-entrance door to the I.S.S. Once you enter the I.S.S., you will go through a decompression chamber, and then you can shed your outer space suits for a while, until the whole party of astronauts get there. So now enjoy the space flight around the world, signing out Mission Control."

"Roger that," said Pilot Walker, as he turned the microphone switches off to mission control. Pilot walker announced to his crew, "Ok crew break out the bubbly, and enjoy the sights."

Malone replied, "I wish I could open a bottle of Champaign in this weightlessness that would be a feat."

Jeremiah looks out the window and says, "Looks like we have company at twelve o' clock."

"Pilot Walker replies, "That's just the Chinese Space Cruiser, they are bringing up the rear in the landing order on the I.S.S. The Russian space cruiser is right behind us, and the European Cruiser behind them." Then the Japanese, French and Canadians to follow."

Maurice said, "Well, it's good to see everyone made it up here safely."

Meanwhile, back on the ground, the Friday evening newspapers are headlining, "Seven Space Cruisers reach space successfully." "The Americans lead the way for peace." "International Space Walk for Peace' set for Saturday."

On the evening world new report, they take an in-depth look at all twelve astronauts from their childhood days to their current mission.

It's a well-covered story that goes into China, Japan, Europe, France, and Canada.

This worldwide event is unraveling in every part of the world with tensions high across the countries.

There is a lot of posturing from all the world powers, on military might and global economy. All the countries involved are imposing embargos and boycotts over nuclear arms, and there seems to be no solution.

That's where these twelve astronauts come in. They are making a last-ditch effort to ease tension between these countries, and to bring the world together, The World News reports.

"We go to the news clip at the White House for a statement from the Chief of Staff. His comment was, "It's really nice to see what our astronauts are doing up there, risking their lives."

"I'll tell you the truth, with these other foreign leaders holding tough on their views and threats, I don't care if they walk on the moon, I don't think it will change their minds."

"There you are, straight from The Chief of Staff, and it pretty much shows the gridlock in world leader views and agendas."

"With the US dollar down and the debt ceiling going through the roof, it is getting our creditors very uneasy, and posturing to come to terms with the world economy."

"Let's just hope they see their astronauts, arm in arm with ours up there, and look in the mirror, then ask themselves, why can't they come to an agreement?" "Signing off, Steve Spencer, World News Tonight."

We then go to the International Space Station, where the welcoming crew is awaiting the Genesis One maiden voyage landing.

They have their work cut out, as they need to make sure all seven space cruisers land, unload their payload, then take back off and return to Earth. The flight deck crew is awaiting Genesis One to come in, with their flags and laser beams.

As soon as they are assembled on the runway, Genesis One comes over the horizon for its maiden landing. What a sight to see from the runway deck, a white flying machine, just floating like a cloud, making its way for landing.

"Mission Control to Genesis One, can you read me?"

"Loud and clear," says Pilot Walker.

"Ok, you are about to come in for a perfect landing, just follow my prompts."

"Go ahead," Pilot Walker says.

Mission Control: "Ok, shut down your rocket boosters, and power your main engine to gear one."

Pilot Walker; "Rocket boosters shut, and main engine turned down."

Mission Control; Ok, now drop your wheels down.

Pilot walker instructs Maurice to push the green button to drop the wheels, and Maurice obliged. "Wheels are down Mission Control," says Pilot Walker.

Mission Control; "Ok, Genesis one, now you are going to match your alignment bar on your guide control with the neon line on the runway, then you're to shut your main engine off, and coast in like a glider. Once you touch down, a tension wire on the runway will catch your spacecraft and bring you to stop."

"Roger that," says Pilot Walker.

The Space Cruiser shuts down its engine, and cruises in for a perfect landing.

Mission control left its microphone on, and the whole crew of six on the Genesis one heard the people at mission control celebrating. Adam turned to everyone, and said with his "John Wayne" voice, "Well look at that, they send us out to pasture, and when we get here, they throw a shindig."

Maurice says, "Darn my legs need some stretching, let's go take a walk."

Pilot walker says, "Not so fast, we need instruction from Mission Control to leave the ship."

Colonel Sullivan gets on the mic and says, "Ok lady and gents, you will leave the cruiser one by one. As you exit the cruiser, you will shoulder clamp on to the tether wire, and slowly pull yourselves to the entrance door. Once you get there, there will be a chamber to enter for air decompression. Once the decompression door opens, you can remove your outer suits, and enter the waiting lounge. Welcome to the new and improved International Space Station."

So, the crew of five exits the space cruiser one by one as instructed, and they all make it into the lounge waiting area.

"Mission control to Pilot Walker,"

"Go mission control."

"There are two astronauts that have been working here for the past two months that need to return with you."

"Roger that mission control."

"Ok, your Space Cruiser is refueling, and your crew are coming aboard. In T-240, you will be taking off headed back to Earth, as we wait for the other six Space Cruisers to land." "Yes Sir," Pilot Walker replies.

Just then we go into the waiting lounge where the five astronauts are.

Adam says, "Check this joint out, a nice TV monitor of the runway here, we can watch the other space cruisers come in.

Malone said, "Is that a bathroom over there, I need to go, I didn't feel too comfortable pissing in my pants."

Maurice just laughed and said, "Well you better get used to it, we could be space walking for a long time."

Up on the monitor, you could see Genesis One taking off with Pilot Walker, and crew. As the U.S. Space Cruiser leaves the runway, the Russian space cruiser pulls in.

"Look," says Eve. "The Russian space cruiser is landing. Adam do you know how to speak Russian?"

"Just the basics Eve, I can certainly welcome him when he comes in."

"That would be a nice gesture Adam."" Let's all welcome him as he comes in," said Maurice.

The Russian space cruiser Lands successfully, then the Russian astronaut pulled his way into the decompression chamber. Once the door opens, he meets the five U.S. astronauts.

"Privyet" said Adam, to his Russian comrade. "Privet am slishkom," replied the Russian cosmonaut.

"Welcome to the I.S.S," said Maurice, as he motions to the place they are standing. The Russian cosmonaut nods at Maurice, letting him know what he meant and shakes his hand.

"His name is Dmitri S. Federoff," says Eve. "He is an accomplished cosmonaut. He was a commander in the Russian military, and he has multiple honors."

"Sounds like you have the hots for him," said Adam.

"Not a chance Adam, I don't mix business with pleasure, but of course you wouldn't know much about that standard." "Oooooooh" said Maurice, "She got you again rookie."

Well, as the Russian cosmonaut became acquainted with the rest of the American astronauts, Malone mentions, "look up at the screen, we now have the European Space Cruiser coming in."

Then he said, "I believe there is a German and a Brit on that space cruiser."

So, they watched the Russian Space Cruiser leave, and the European Cruiser land. After a few minutes the decompression chamber doors opened, and the two European astronauts appeared.

"Well hello, it's our American counterparts, look chum our Russian counterpart is here also," said the British astronaut.

The German said, "Die Japaner sind direkt vor unserer Schwanz," in German.

"Which means the Japanese were right on our tail, and they should be landing shortly," said the Brit.

"Please allow me to introduce my partner and myself to all. My partner from the German space agency, that will accompany us on this mission, is the one and only Mr. Axel P. Klein. You may call him Axel, and last but not least the pleasure is mine, at introducing myself as Mr. Charles G. Jones." Yes, you may call me Charlie."

Sure enough, on the monitor you can see the European cruiser leaving and The Japanese cruiser landing.

"Konnichiwa," said the Japanese Astronaut, as he came through the decompression doors.

"And Konnichiwa to you," said Jeremiah.

Adam asked Jeremiah "When did you learn Japanese Surfer Dude?"

Jeremiah replied, "Don't you know anything Cowboy?"

Whenever a foreigner greets you in a different language, you repeat what they say back. This way if they are calling you an asshole, you're just returning the compliment."

"Hey, that's pretty smart surfer dude," said Adam.

"So, you must be Mr. Haruto L. Tanaka?" says Eve.

"Tadashii," says Haruto.

"Tanaka" says Adam.

"Tadashii says Haruto."

"Tanaka" says Adam.

"Tadashii," says Haruto.

Oh, never mind, how about we call you Harry?"

Then the Japanese astronaut looks at Adam strangely and throws his hand up, and replies. "O K."

Adam then points to him and says, "You can call me Cowboy." Haruto slowly says," Coowboi"

"Yes, that's it," Adam says with a smile.

Right about then you could see the Japanese Space Cruiser leave, and the French Space Cruiser land.

"The French are coming," says Malone. Just a few minutes later French Astronaut Mr. Jacques R. Dubois comes in. "Salute," said the Frenchman, as he walked through the door.

"Hello and welcome," said Maurice as he walked up to greet him.

"Mon copain canadien est juste derrière moi," said the Frenchman." "Sounds like you said your Canadian friend is just behind you." "Oui," the French astronaut replied.

"I knew that French class in high school would come in handy one day," said Maurice.

Now there were ten astronauts in the waiting lounge. The room was almost at max capacity, as the crowd was waiting on the last two astronauts to arrive.

An announcement came over the TV monitor, "Welcome all to the International Space Station, we are happy to see you all, or at least most of you at this point."

"While we wait for the next two arrivals, please feel free to use the restrooms, and there are refreshment dispensers for you to enjoy. Once the Canadian and Chinese Space Cruisers drop off their astronauts, we will be back to direct you along with this mission. Thank you and see you then."

Just then, you could see the French cruiser leave, and the Canadian cruiser land.

A few minutes pass, and the decompression doors open.

The Canadian astronaut says, "Bonjour a tous il heureux d'être ici avec vous."

Maurice replied once again to the French speaking Canadian, "Well it's great to have you here, welcome to the group."

Jeremiah asks Maurice "Can you ask him his name?"

Maurice asked; "Comment vous appelez-vous?"

The Canadian replied, "Let me introduce myself "My name is Alexandre H. Roy."

"Well, look here, the Canadian is bilingual."

"Hey Alexandre, do you know any Chinese so we can make the next guy feel at home?" Adam asked.

Alexandre replies "No, sorry pal, just two languages is all I can handle."

"By the way, just call me Alex."

"Alex, I always liked that name," said Eve.

Adam replied, "Watch her Alex, she's a snake in the grass."

Alex asked Eve, "What did he mean by that?"

She replied, "Awe, he's just mad I gave him a bite of the apple."

Alex laughed. "Oh, I get it, Adam, Eve, apple, and snake, which was very clever."

Adam replied, "I told you, you need to watch her."

The whole room cheered looking up at the monitor as the Canadian Space Cruiser pulled off, and the last Space Cruiser from China was landing.

I think they were just getting their selves all pumped up for the upcoming spacewalk. Just then, the door opened for the final time, as astronaut Zhang K. Chen steps through.

Before he can get a word out, he gets a welcome mob all around him, as if he just hit a home run to win the World Series.

As the group gets excited, Adam yells, "Hail, hail the gangs all here!" Then the crowd joined in singing," What the hell do we care, what the hell do we care. Hail, hail the gangs all here, what the hell do we care now!"

"After a few minutes, the crowd settled down, for an announcement that came over the TV. "Welcome all, to the "International Space Walk for Peace.""

"Now that everyone is here, let me introduce myself as Jack Parsons. I will be your mission guide."

"As you all came through the decompression chamber, you shed your space suits. We put them in a safe place for your departures. You will adorn a new space suit, designed for everyone to wear matching suits. Every suit will have a small patch of your origin country's flag."

"That will be the only difference telling your suits apart. This will show solidarity between all of you, showing your countries you are all united."

"There is an audience of seven billion people that will watch you walk out that station door. One hundred forty-two media satellites are focused on your walk."

"You are the focus of an international world peace movement, starting all around the world down there. You are the threads keeping this unsettling world united in millions of eyes down there. You all will be in the history books for doing what you are doing."

"You should have the honor and be proud of what you stand for. The way this mission will work will need full cooperation from all of you."

"You will all get an exclusive tour of the new space station while our crew makes preparation for your walk. Once we finish the tour, all astronauts are to report to the staging area in wing B."

"This will be the area where you can use the restroom and will also be a dressing area for you to put on your space suits."

"Once everyone is suited up, you will one by one, exit the space station spacewalk door."

"Once you step out the door, you will take your shoulder hook, and hook it onto the tether wire waiting for you."

"Your name will be announced around the world, but you won't be able to hear it.

The order of the walk will follow as, The American astronauts will step out first, then the Russian cosmonaut, then the Japanese, German, British, French, Canadian, and finally the Chinese astronaut."

"Once all astronauts are out on their tether wires, they will join hands for the entire world to see and document. You will need to hold hands for about 10 minutes to show solidarity. Then once all the cameras are off you can relax, and rotate positions to come in, and take a break. Only two on a break at a time."

"This walk can last for weeks. So, this will take a lot of dedication. Now if your walk can bring world leaders together, with all the worlds public support, you all will be world heroes. The longer you walk together for peace, the more pressure the public will put on their government leaders."

"Ok, now let's get started. If everyone can walk in single file down the hallway to your left, I will start you on a tour of this space station. We will start by exiting the room you are in and following the red line on the walls." "You will feel weightlessness while traveling throughout the space station. We will start with the labs, then to the control rooms, then take a look at the docks, and so on."

All twelve astronauts went on their space station tour getting ready to do the walk. The five Americans stayed together. The French and Canadian paired off. The Japanese and Chinese stayed together, and the Brit, Russian, and German grouped together for the tour.

While the gang went on their tour, the stage was set for one of the greatest statements.

The world was gearing up to broadcast live on the Five o'clock news. Every media outlet was covering this story.

Adam says to Maurice," This is a crazy thing we are about to do."

Maurice replies, "Yea somebody needs to do it."

Jeremiah pinched in, "Yea, I can't believe all this political bullshit between all these countries. Everything can be worked out. I hope this walk opens somebody's eyes."

As they are finishing up the tour, Jack Parsons says, "Let's all take a right into the staging area in wing B."

"This is where you all can relax before dressing for the big show. It's our kind of version of The Green Room." So, the five American astronauts enter the room first, then the others follow in.

Malone says, "This is the biggest room on the station."

Eve replies, "Yea, and check it out, there's another TV in here with a view of the spacewalk exit door."

Adam replies, "That T.V. is the coverage of the media watching us, as we go out that door."

By now all the astronauts are in the room, just talking among their selves, trying to make out what each other are saying.

"There is a big communication gap in this room," says Eve.

"Yea, one thing they didn't think about when they were planning this mission. Just one tiny little detail," Maurice replies.

Adam chuckled. "Well, if you think about it, who needs communication when you're just floating out there in the stars, looking at Mother Earth."

"The Walk"

The announcement came over the telecom in the room. "All astronauts, one at a time, enter in the dressing area to be fitted with your space exploration suit."

Adam then pointed to Eve and said, "Ladies first." Eve then stood up and walked to the dressing area. Then the rest followed.

In New York City, they are broadcasting this event on the big screen in Times Square, also in China's Tiananmen Square, at the Gate of Heavenly People. They are broadcasting in Germany at Alexanderplatz, the biggest public gathering in Berlin. There are people gathering all over the world in support for these twelve astronaut's missions.

Back in the states, people mass in the streets of every big city, wearing t-shirts labeled "Space Walk for Peace."

The police are putting barricades up all over the nation, protecting national monuments, and other government buildings. There is an outcry of local government support.

Mayors of major cities are making press conferences, urging protestors to protest without violence. This whole event worldwide is snowballing out of control. The peaceful factions of the world are making a stand against world fighting. The newspaper headlines read, "The sleeping giant of peace has awoken."

Back at the International Space Station in the staging area, all five American astronauts are fully dressed in their space exploration suits with the Russian cosmonaut. There are still six more left to get dressed. Eve says, "Now I'm getting nervous.

We are about to step out into space, and the only thing keeping us from floating in space for infinity is one little tether cable."

Adam says, "Don't worry Jersey Girl, you have all these strong men to protect you."

Maurice said, "Don't worry Eve, they have you going out there in the middle of the four of us, so you will have two of us on each side, in case anything goes wrong."

Eve said, "Thanks guys, that was so relieving to hear." The Japanese astronaut was dressing with the German astronaut.

In France, the public is gathering at all popular squares like Place Charles de Gaulle, Place Dauphine, and Place de Furstenberg. In Japan, the public is gathering in Shanghai, and other parts all to watch this event. By now, back at the space station, all the astronauts are dressed and ready to exit into space.

Back at Mission Control in Houston, they are patching in their audio to all the media satellites, so their introduction of the astronauts goes live worldwide, and all video of the event is linked worldwide. The crowds are gathering in London, and all the cities in England. Everyone is watching TV, on the event about to unfold.

The world is excited, and united to see those astronauts walk through that door.

The astronauts are all ready, as the guide asked them to stand at the back wall to get a photo of the whole group together.

All the astronauts set up for a picture, and the photographer snaps the first couple pictures. "Great job all," says guide Jack Parsons.

"Well, the time is now to get out there, and show the world who you are. I need everyone to get in a single file line to the spacewalk door. You all know your positions, with you Maurice, leading the walk."

All the astronauts get ready to walk.

Guide Parsons says, "Remember everyone, once you step through, hook your shoulder hook to the lifeline tether wire."

The gang of astronauts get rallied up again, as the Russian and German lead the group with the same tune, "Hail, hail, the gangs all here, what the hell do we care." These astronauts have been training for this for over a year in their countries.

Adam shouts in his," John Wayne voice," The time has come partners, to walk the walk, and talk the talk." They all are jubilant and ready to go.

"Hello, all the world, I am Steve Gault of channel 10 news in Houston."

"We are live here in Houston Texas, at the Johnson Space Center. We are the Mission Control of flight operations, where we are televised live all over the world, as we wait for the countdown to the first annual Space Walk for Peace."

Just then up at the space station, the five Americans were gathering near the door, to exit with Maurice leading the way.

Adam is right behind him and says, "Hey Islander, don't forget to hook to the lifeline pal. Maurice replies, "I got this Cowboy," as he reaches to open the door.

"Welcome world, to the Two Thousand Twenty, Space Walk for Peace. Get ready as the countdown begins. 10, 9, 8, 7, 6, 5, 4, 3, 2, 1," and the door is opening."

"Ladies and gentlemen, our first astronaut to step through the door, is an American astronaut, Mission Commander, Maurice Kalu." Maurice steps through the door, and reaches up and hooks his shoulder strap, then floats in space, as he can feel the eyes of the world watching him.

Down on the ground there are outpours of cheers from the Earth, hoping that the astronaut can hear them. Maurice floats down the line so the next astronaut can exit.

"Next out the door is another American astronaut, Mission Specialist, Adam Pinkert" The cameras are flashing, as Adam steps out with his arm positioned with his thumbs up signal, as he grabs the line and floats down alongside Maurice.

Adam talks in his helmet, "Mom if you could see me now."

"Next out the door is another American astronaut, Mission Specialist Eve S. McGovern."

Eve steps through the door, and hooks her shoulder clip and let's go, then screams "Yeeeeeeah!," as she floats down the line next to Adam.

"Next out the door is yet another American Astronaut, Mission Specialist Malone Akbar." Malone steps out hooks up, and floats down the line besides Eve.

"One more American is walking out the door as we speak, and it is Astronaut Lieutenant Colonel Jeremiah Edelman."

Jeremiah is the last American to step out of the space station door. He hooks up, and floats down the line to make room for the next astronaut. The TV newscaster says, "Let's give a big hand to the five Americans as they float together in space." There are cheers all around the hometowns of the newly dubbed, "Fab Five."

As soon as the five Americans were out the door, the announcer started again for the first Russian Cosmonaut.

Mission Specialist Dmitri Federoff. Dimetri steps out, and hooks on to the tether line, as he floats down next to Jeremiah. "Let's give a hand to our representative from Russia." The crowds in Russia applaud.

"Next out the door is the Japanese Astronaut Lieutenant HarutoTanaka." Haruto hooks himself to the tether, and floats down next to Demetri. The announcer once again, "Let's gives a hand to our Japanese astronaut." Then the crowds in Japan go nuts.

"Ok, next out the door is the first of two, from the European Space team, with the German astronaut exiting first, and his name is Colonel Axel Klein." Axel takes his position, and floats down in line. The T.V. announcer announces, "Let's give a big hand to our German astronaut." All the people in Germany rejoice.

"It's the ninth astronaut coming out of the space station door, and it's the second one from the European Space Team. It's the British astronaut Charles Jones." Charlie hooks up, and floats down next to his German partner. The announcer speaks; "Let's give a big hand to our British astronaut." All of Brittan erupts in joy."

"Next is the tenth astronaut coming through the door. It's the French Astronaut Lieutenant Jacques Dubois." Mr. Dbois then hooks to the tether, and floats on down next to the Brit. The TV announcer announces "Let's give a big hand to our French astronaut." All of France is jubilant and erupts in cheers.

"The eleventh astronaut coming through the door. It's the Canadian Astronaut Alexandre Roy."

Alexandre hooks up and grabs the tether line as he floats down. The T.V. announcer says, "Let's give a hand to our Canadian Astronaut." All of Canada applauds.

The announcer says. "Let the drums roll please as we announce our twelfth astronaut tonight." The drums roll, as the last astronaut emerges from the space station door. "It's the Chinese Astronaut Commander Zhang Chen." Zang grabs the tether, and hooks himself on, and floats down. "The T.V. announcer says, "Let's give a shout out to our friend from China, and all of China erupts yelling Zang, Zang, and Zang.

"This is Steve Galt, and what a pleasure it's been to announce the names of these brave men, and woman who are risking their lives all for the sake of peace. This is the biggest day of my life."

Twelve humans standing together arm in arm, and all the worlds' eyes are watching them as they prepare to link up together holding hand to hand. The announcer says, "Let's all take this time to bow down, and pray to whatever god you believe in, and ask for world peace."

"The Abduction"

As the world takes a moment in silence, the astronauts each other and locking hands together. First the five Americans, then to the Russian, Japanese, the Europeans, the French, the Canadian, and then the last touch the Chinese astronaut's hand. The cameras are rolling now.

All twelve are united, as all the eyes of the world are watching. All the people, all the governments, all the spiritual leaders, and all the astronauts holding hands. Cameras are flashing, and it seemed like everything moved in slow motion. Time was standing still as the astronauts were smiling in slow motion at each other.

Suddenly, there was a frightening presence above, a giant dark shadow appeared over the lights, cameras and astronauts. The astronauts looked up in slow motion, in complete horror at a giant circular disc hovering just over their heads.

This thing was about as round as an Olympic size stadium. It was huge, It was something never seen before, they were in complete shock.

In slow motion, you can see the horror on their faces, as they pull their way back to the space station. As they were scrambling in panic, two giant black tubes lowered down, one from each end of the giant disc, and on each end of the astronaut line. Before they could even start back to the station, these two tubes closed in on the astronauts, and as they drew closer, they were pulling a vacuum. The vacuum was so strong it pulled the astronauts toward them.

The first three Americans on the right, and the Chinese, then Canadian on the left were sucked into the tubes. After about five seconds all the astronauts were pulled so hard from their tether lines. It ripped the hooks right from their shoulder clips.

The entire world's video cameras saw the astronauts being violently ripped from their safety wires, and being spun violently into the great vacuum of the alien spacecraft disc.

The giant tubes withdrew after the last astronaut was last seen, and the alien disc just vanished away. All that was left was the torn remnants of space suits dangling on the tether

The entire world witnessed this live, and the whole world went silent. A silent never heard before, like the world was at complete peace. Everyone was speechless, the crew at mission control, the newscasters, brothers and sisters, mothers and fathers to world leaders. There wasn't anyone on planet Earth that can comprehend what just happened.

Everything and everyone just shut everything down, and quietly went home in disbelief. Everyone witnessed what happened, so there were no questions.

The harsh truth that something, not from our world, just violated everything we as human beings were taught to believe. Like that monster in your dreams when you were a little child, just came back to let you know he was real.

Mission Control in Houston made a brief statement live on the air. Just then Colonel Jack K. Sullivan walks up to the podium. "Ladies and gentlemen, it saddens me to bring you the news of an alien spacecraft, which has captured twelve of the finest astronauts this world has ever seen. We at mission control are in disbelief, and complete shock. We will do everything we can as a human race to see we get these astronauts back to our planet."

"We will work with mission control centers all over the world, and with all the military's tracking devices worldwide."

"I will end this press conference prematurely, to make way from what I believe is, the President of The United States, which is about to take the podium in Washington DC."

T.V. reporter, "Let's switch now to the President"

"Hello to all the men, woman and children of this great nation, and all the people around the world. We have turned a new page in time. We have to add a new chapter to our history books."

"As President, I want to tell you everything is ok, but as you all know, we are dealing here with the unknown."

"Before we can even think about getting the astronauts back, we as leaders of our nations must put everything dividing us to the side temporarily and organize together our technology."

"We must come up with an action plan to protect the human race from this event, and work with the world's mission controls to put a game plan together."

"We must work swift and intelligently."

"I want to warn everyone to take shelter tonight, as I will call an executive order to activate our Navy and Air Force, and put them around our nation, and above our skies on a twenty-four, seven day a week protection force. Protecting our nation and protecting the human race from these unknown forces."

"It will take a lot of effort and communication from our neighboring countries governments. I will end this press conference with you, to get on the phone and make these important phone calls. God Bless and goodnight."

Three hours have passed since the tragic event. The whole world is in shock. The alien believers are rallying in the streets. Shouting, "We told you so, all you non-believers, today is our day."

While onlookers are in disbelief, people are going to their clergy, churches, and religious places all around the world looking for answers.

The whole experience sent the world into temporary shock. The presence of aliens captured on every video outlet in the world was too much for the world to handle. There was chaos in the streets all over the world. Towns were under Marshall Law. It was all an aftermath reaction to the alien presence in modern day times.

Local leaders were scrambling in every town in America, making speeches to assure the local people security from the aliens. It was a real grip on reality.

Meanwhile, light years away aboard the alien spacecraft, Eve was the first to come to and open her eyes. There was just a blurred vision, until it became clear she was strapped in a vertical glass cylinder.

She had noticed her space suit was removed. She looked across the room, and she saw other glass tubes with people in them. That's when it just hit her of what happened to her.

A brisk chill ran down her back from the base of her spine to her tailbone.

She didn't panic when she awoke, she just kept still. The rest of the astronauts awoke, they experienced the same thing, being strapped in a glass tube along the walls of a giant circular room.

"Eve is that you?" She heard in her head. She looked around, and there was no speaker in her tube.

She heard it again, and it was loud and clear. "Eve is that you?" She looked across the room, and in one of the tubes along the wall she saw Adam.

When she focused in on Adam, she replied in her head, "Yes, I'm here," Is you Adam?" And when she heard Adam reply, "Yes it's me," she almost passed out.

The reasoning being she did not speak out loud and she did not open her mouth. She just communicated across the room to Adam using telepathy. This was a lot for her to comprehend.

Adam picked up on what just happened and yelled "This is fucking awesome," out loud in his tube. Adam looked over at the Russian astronaut, and said in his head,

"Hey Dmitry, can you hear me?"

Dmitry responded, "Who's talking to me in Russian?" Dmitry looks around at the glass tubes, and finds Adam staring at him.

"I don't know any Russian, and you just spoke to me in English," said Adam.

"I didn't even open my mouth" said Dmitry.

"This telepathy is the shit," said Adam."

Malone looks over to Maurice and asked, "Where the hell are we?"

"I think we were captured" replied Maurice.

"How do we have the ability to communicate in telepathy?' asked Malone. "Your guess is as good as mine," Surfer Dude.

The Chinese astronaut looked through his glass at the British astronaut and thought,

"Hey Charlie, are you ok?"

The Brit said, "When the hell did you learn English Zhang?"

"About fifteen minutes ago," said Zang.

"Dam, I didn't even open my mouth, I was just thinking that question at you," said the British astronaut.

"It's kind of crazy you are talking in Chinese," said Zang.

The German astronaut looks at the Brit and says, "This place is creeping me out."

The Brit says, "Well we are not dead yet, so they obviously need something from us."

Axel the German astronaut replied, "That's what I am afraid of, I don't have any spare parts to give."

The astronauts were in a giant rounded room with 12 glass tubes holding them around the walls of the room.

There was a circular ceiling over the room with greenish blue lighting.

"What the hell happened to us?" Eve questioned Adam, through telepathy.

Adam looked at Maurice and thought, "How the hell do I know?"

Maurice replied without saying a word to Eve or Adam, "Looks like we are captured by an alien spacecraft. It seems when we were doing the Space Walk for Peace, that's when they captured us. My memory is a little fuzzy on that though."

The French astronaut looks at Maurice and thinks "You are right Maurice; I remember getting sucked up into giant tubes."

The Chinese add in," Yes I also remember the giant spin we succumbed to.

Adam thinks, "We are all having the same conversation in our heads. It seems if we are looking at someone, we can pick up what they are talking about, and hear everyone else in that thought."

Jeremiah looks at Adam and thinks "Yea, this is some crazy shit we have to get used to. What is that round gold disc in the center of the room on the floor?"

Adam thinks, "Yea and the railing around the disc,"

The Russian looks at Adam and thinks. "Can everyone breathe ok?"

Maurice looks at the Russian and thinks, "Yea, there seems to be oxygen supplied in these tubes were in."

"I wonder how long we were out, and how far we are away from Earth," thought the Japanese Astronaut as he looked at Malone.

"I guess we will find out real soon, why we were taken, and what they want with us." Malone communicated back to the Japanese astronaut.

"They took our space suits, when did they do that?" Eve thinks.

"Who knows what they had done to us before we awoke, I feel fine it doesn't seem like they harmed us at all," Malone replied through telepathy.

All of the sudden the dark areas of the walls between the glass tubes were illuminated, and behind the glass walls it seemed there were about 25 aliens walking around. Some were manning control centers, and others were just looking through the glass, trying to get a peek at the captured astronauts.

Eve freaked out, and verbally screamed in her glass tube.

The Russian looked at the Chinese astronaut, and tele- communicated to him, "Don't move Zang, there is one right next to your tube."

Adam looked at the Russian, and tele- communicated, "Look at these little shit's, peeking around like we are animals in a cage. They look like the aliens we captured in Roswell."

As soon as Adam thought that thought, all the aliens stopped, and looked at him like they knew what he was thinking, and they could relate to an alien from area fifty-one.

"Whoops, looks like I'll never mention that guy again," Adam thinks to himself. After that thought left Adam, the aliens went on their business to do various duties controlling the spacecraft.

"It looks like some kind of a control room," tele-communicated the German.

"Yea it seems like this level we are on is their control level, the little pea sized bastards," tele-communicated the French astronaut.

"Yes it's a little weird but they don't seem to be aggressive, the little buggers, also out of all the alien movies I watched, who would think the real ones would be the little flesh colored ones with the big heads, skinny little bodies and big black eyes?" tele- communicated Maurice.

"It's the same description of aliens drawn throughout centuries on cave walls to modern artwork. It's almost like we knew who these guys or gals were all along," tele-communicated Eve.

The German looks at Maurice and thinks "Ok let me get this right now. We know who captured us, we're on a fucking alien spaceship with these little fuckers, and we don't know what they want from us. Suddenly, we could talk to each other, by not saying a fucking word to each other. We don't know how long we have been gone. We know our countries can't put out a search and rescue for us. We could be fucking light years away. Oh guys, we are in one big ball of shit,"

Maurice tele-communicates to the German with his thoughts. "Ok, let's not push the panic button yet.

We are captured, but we are still alive. We need to keep cool heads, and we must stick together in this alien environment. Yes, they showed us who they are. They don't seem violent. They already handled us, to get our space suits off, and put us in these tubes, and yet they harmed none of us doing so."

"We have to be positive here and take one thing at a time." "Don't think of all the negative things at once."

Just then, the illuminated glass panels between the tubes, slowly dimmed to dark so they could no longer see the alien space crew. The Chinese astronaut tele-communicates to himself, "Boy I'm getting tired of standing here, I wish something would happen, the suspense is killing me. I'm getting hungry, and I can use something to drink."

The French astronaut looks at the China man and tele-communicates, "Yea boy, I could go for a nice American cheeseburger."

Adam looks at the French guy and tele-communicates, "Hey how about some French fries with that burger?" and chuckles. The French astronaut tele-communicates back to Adam "Ah, we have a comedian on board with us people."

The German looks at them two and tele-communicates, "Hey you two, smarten up. We need to get serious here. We're on a fucking alien spaceship. We can't be joking around here."

Adam tele-communicates his thought to the German, "Lighten your loafers," with his John Wayne thoughts, which are better sounding than his real voice.

"You know if I we're one of those aliens, and I ran across a mean spirited little shit like you, well you know I would pick you out of the bunch, and make an example out of you to the rest, on how not to act."

The German mumbled something to himself and backed down. "OK, guys, let's all settle down and think with cool heads.

I got a feeling any minute, they will try to communicate with us, and the last thing we need to show them we can't get along with each other," Maurice tele-communicates at the two.

"Maurice is right, we need to stick together like the team we were on that spacewalk. After all this is why we are here.

Our countries could not see eye to eye, so we set out to be an example of peace between countries. It's one for all, and all for one. Maurice will be our leader from this point forward," tele-communicated the China man.

The British Astronaut looks at Maurice, and thinks, "If you're our new leader then what kind of plans do you have for all of us to get out of here?

Maurice tele-communicates his thoughts, "My British counterpart and friend, let's be patient here, and observe our surroundings. Let's see what exactly we are up against and communicate with each other on a plan to escape."

"Right now, I think we have a visitor coming, and I also think he can hear exactly what is going on in our heads.

So, let's think good thoughts, and make our visitor think we are just a bunch of happy chaps."

"The Encounter"

Everyone noticed the circular gold disc, with the railing around it in the center of the floor, was lowering down slowly. As the disc was lowered out of view a glass tube, the size of the hole rose up, until it stood about six foot from the floor. The tube had a dome shaped top making the tube enclosed. Then once the tube was standing, it filled up with a slightly blue gas.

The astronauts watched silently, as the sight of a big head alien was rising up into the gas filled tube. He was the same alien they saw earlier behind the glass walls. Big head, black slanting eyes, small mouth, ear holes with no lobes, small flat chest, skinny arms and legs and no genitalia. The one thing familiar was his skin. It was flesh colored and looked like human skin.

As soon as the alien was standing flush with the floor level in the bluish glass tube, the lights in the room dimmed, and the tubes that the astronauts were in illuminated. The glass tube the alien was in illuminated also.

There was a theater like effect with the audience in the background, surrounding the main attraction in the middle. The alien looked to his left, and slowly eyed up every astronaut from left to right. The astronauts were in awe. They were shocked with eyes wide open. The alien spoke to all the astronauts using telepathy,

"Welcome my guest, or should I say my chosen ones."

"We are Soulfurians, we are from the planet Soulfuria, a planet ten times bigger than your Sun, with an atmosphere of Nitrogen gas. We are two black hole travel distances, between our planet, and your solar system. We have been patrolling space for billions of your years. We are the takers and the givers of life forms in the universes, and galaxies".

"We are the keepers of the universes. I'm sure you all have many questions."

"When we captured you, we used vacuum tubes, that are designed to spin you up to unconsciousness, and while doing that, it forced a lot of blood pressure to a certain area of your brains."

"Until it ruptured a membrane, and it allowed blood flow to an area of the brain, that humans have not developed yet. We developed telepathy billions of your years ago."

"This is why we have no lobes on our ears, and why our mouths are small. This my human friends, is why we are communicating in telepathy at this moment."

"We needed to do this, for us to communicate with you." Adam is the first to answer back, "Well that answers one question that's been bugging all of us."

The Chinese Astronaut Zang looks at the alien, and tele-communicates, "You say you are the keepers of the universes, meaning more than one universe?"

The alien tele-communicates, "Yes we are the keepers of all the universes, and there are an infinite number of them in the Cosmos. You see when the big bang happened, our planet was the first to develop billions of your years ago. We come back from time and space and move forward to the newer galaxies."

"This is the reason for our existence. We have existed way before your solar system and planets were formed. We handle all changes of life form on the planet you call Earth. We control all life form existence in all universes. We make sure the life forms we create flourish and thrive. We do this by managing energies called "Starsouls.""

Malone looks at the Alien and tele-communicates, "What are these Starsouls you mentioned?"

"In a few minutes, I will demonstrate the function of Starsouls. We live for about one hundred thousand of your years to every one of ours. We were the first life formed in the cosmos. We are every living thing's keeper."

Eve looked at the alien and tele-communicates "So that would make you Spangels, (translation space angels)."

The Alien tele-communicated back, "That's a good way of putting it. You can call me Spangel."

"Why are we here, and why are we being strapped like this in tubes?" tele-communicated by Jeremiah.

The Soulfurian looked at Jeremiah, "Oh well, you see those tubes that you're in are just transporters to move you from one level to another, and those straps on your arms and legs are just Velcro, to keep you from falling over while you were sleeping. If you pull hard enough, they will just pull right off."

Just then there was the sound of Velcro straps ripping all over the room, as the astronauts wrestled to be at ease in their tubes.

"There are three levels to this spaceship. The one where I lifted up from, is the same one you were down in. On that level, we take in supplies and planet samples.

Also, that level is where we exit the spaceship. That is the level we vacuumed you from space, and removed your space suits, and put them away for departure."

"That is the Acceptance and Departure level. This level we are on now is the Control and Living Quarter's level."

"This is where all fifty Soulfurian crew members work in the control room, and where all the sleeping quarters are."

"The top level has a giant glass dome and is called the Observance Level. It has a 180-degree space, sky view."

The Russian astronaut looked at the alien and tele-communicated, "You mentioned you put our suits away for a future departure. Does that mean you will not kill us, and return us to our planet?"

"In time, if everything goes well, we do plan to return you as messengers to your people. The why you are here is a little more detailed. Right now, we have other planet missions to take care of. So, I will let everyone get rest, and let it soak in your memories what just happened to you."

"When you return, we will discuss Starsouls, and why you are with us. The door behind you in each of your tubes, is the door to your resting quarters. Each has a bed, lamp, a cooling box with human refreshments, and each unit has a bathroom for cleansing."

"There are changes of clothing you will wear while on this ship, located in the dresser in your room."

"Once in your rooms, you will notice all walls are hermetically sealed, with a constant supply of the right mix of Nitrogen & Oxygen."

"There is no possible contact with your planet Earth. "Also, don't even think about escape. We are Soulfurians, we breathe Nitrogen gas like you breathe, but with no oxygen. So, besides your quarters, and when we fill the third level with oxygen, the rest of the ship is infused with a Nitrogen gas mixture that would make you sleepy. Now it's time to go to your quarters and return in a couple of your hours."

"After we are finished with our planetary checks, you will return to your transporters dressed in the ships uniforms and be mentally rested for more intelligence sessions. When you hear the buzzers go off, you will have fifteen minutes to return to your transporting tubes. As you humans would say it "go take a cat nap."

"Thank you, thanks a lot," were thoughts tele-communicated from the astronauts to the alien that Eve nicknamed Spangel, as they all were turning, and retiring to their quarters."

Eve turns to open the door behind her to reveal her quarters. The door opens, and sure enough it looked like an upscale prison cell with a soft bedding material never seen before.

It was airy fluff matting. She walked to the bathroom, as her tired eyes were looking at a toilet, a wash basin, and a stall shower.

She thought to herself, "Well I guess the plumbing has not changed in a billion years."

She opened the small dresser drawer, and sure enough there was clothing in the drawer. She picked it up to find it was exactly her size. Wondering immediately, how long have these aliens been scoping me out? The jumper suit she was looking at was the same color blue as the alien's gas mixture. She thought to herself, "Great they want us to look like them, I'm surprised they don't leave us a giant pair of black sunglasses."

Well she was so tired, she just pulled off her flight suit, and just plopped down in bed.

As she lay in bed, she thought to herself, this is the weirdest thing I have ever been through, but somehow, I feel this will turn out ok. "Well, I should just wait for the buzzer," she says while falling asleep.

The other eleven astronauts didn't take long to fall asleep. They were the heroes two days ago in the eyes of the world, on their way to the other end of the universe, in an alien spacecraft. They were in no immediate danger, napping while cruising the cosmos.

The astronauts went to sleep thinking, where in the cosmos did their countries think they were? What did their mission controls think happened to them? Did anyone believe they were alive? What were their countries doing back home?

Back on the home front planet Earth, all the countries of the world were scrambling for national defense from the invading aliens.

In the United States, the President gave an executive order to bring all US military from around the world back to surround its borders and commanded the Navy and Air force to patrol the skies in case of an alien attack.

Because of this, it started jubilation all over the world to rid the U.S. military from their countries. It was the same for Brittan, Germany, Japan, France, Russia,

Canada and China. They all had their warplanes in the skies protecting their own countries. They all had their militaries protecting their borders.

It was a call for human defense. The leaders of all countries are about to hold a summit on temporary world peace. The summit puts the differences between them on hold until the alien crises is over, or until they learn the fate of their twelve astronauts. "Let's listen in on a speech from the U.S. President," announced the TV newscaster from Boulder Colorado.

"Ladies, gentlemen and fellow countrymen, we are gathered here today to address the events that happened in the past few days."

"As you all know, starting with the International Spacewalk for Peace tragedy, we learn that we are not alone in the cosmos. So after speaking with world leaders, we have come to an agreement to put our differences a side, until this situation comes to an end."

"We will implement a general alert system that will be broadcast daily on the possible alien return risk."

"We are watching the skies worldwide, and as soon as there is any kind of threat, there will be alarms sounding."

"When you hear these alarms, do not panic. Just calmly return to your homes until we verify what set the alarm, and tune into your local newscast for updates. Do not rush to schools, if your children are in session. All school personnel will take care of them until further notice.

Thank you, and remember we are defending you."

Pro alien people are coming out from every corner of the planet. Mostly young people, and older people from the sixties' era.

In the Middle East, the people are in the streets, with picture signs of alien heads with a number one next to them, and a picture of the US president head with a zero next to it.

They feel the alien presence made the U.S. and its allies pull their troops out of their countries. It seems worldwide, the alien presence put everyone at ease on one hand and put everyone in fear of them returning on the other hand.

It was a time for mixed emotions with the clergy, on explaining alien presence in their faiths, except for the oldest faith in mankind, the Hindu faith.

Although they do not worship aliens, they have a general belief in them. It is Buddhist belief there is other life out in the cosmos also. One of the twelve astronauts, the China man Zang is a Buddhist believer and the American Jeremiah follows Hinduism faith.

Also, the Japanese astronaut is a Buddhist/Shinto believer. Astronaut Adam Pinkert believes in Judaism, two others are Muslim and Protestant, and astronaut Eve McGovern is a Christian. So even upon the alien spacecraft there is a vast mixture of religious beliefs. That was one requirement of making the "Space Walk for Peace."

The Soulfurian space craft is now in the next galaxy from the Milky Way galaxy. The astronauts have been fast asleep, as the Soulfurian crew navigates the other planets in the next galaxy.

The leader of the Soulfurians, that Eve nicknamed Spangel, will give the astronauts about two hours of rest before the next intelligence session.

The Soulfurians will finish their mission by then, and will head back past the Milky Way, on their way back home to their planet Soulfuria.

As the buzzer sounds, it startles the twelve astronauts. One by one they jump out of bed, and dress into the blue jumpsuits, their Soulfurian host called for.

Then most went to their washroom, and either freshened up, or just slapped water on their face as they rushed to get back to their transport tubes. Once they were all in their tubes, the leader Soulfurian raised from the lower level up onto the level the astronauts were.

"STARSOULS"

"Welcome back chosen ones, just when you thought this was a dream, you find you are living the dream of cosmic visitors." "We are about to enter back to your hometown Milky Way galaxy, only to show you what we mean by Starsouls. I will transfer you up to the third level, where you will be free to roam around in the observatory section of the spacecraft. We just infused the area with oxygen for easy breathing. I will raise my glass enclosed dome up to meet you all."

As the twelve transport tubes lifted up, the Soulfurian's tube lifted up through the center floor of the third level. Once on that level, the astronauts opened the transport doors, and walked freely in the glass domed room. It was a circular room with a glass dome that went all the way around the room from floor to ceiling. They were all a little off balance, because it looked like they were spacewalking again.

It was a spectacular sight of the Milky Way galaxy they were looking at.

Adam spoke for the first time "We don't need telepathy in here."

Then the French astronaut looked at Adam and tele-communicated, "Since I don't speak your English, we will still need telepathy to communicate."

Eve then said, "Home sweet home. If only they knew we were looking down at them and we were ok." The German, British, and Japanese, were all circling around the Soulfurians nitrogen gas infused glass tube, like he was an attraction.

'Starsouls," The Soulfurian tele- communicated to all the astronauts to get their attention.

"A Starsoul is the center of everything living." All the astronauts gave the alien better attention after hearing that.

"What we as Soulfurians want to accomplish here is to take the nonbelievers in all of you and make you all believers in our truth."

"Then we want you to go back to your origins, and pass our truth onto your leaders and people, like modern day prophets, spreading our truth." Now the astronauts had their full attention on the Alien.

"Consider you taking care of a fish tank or aquarium," communicated the Spangel. You add whatever live fish, or coral or plants, and do everything in your power to keep that environment alive."

"Yet if something goes wrong threatening life in general in that fish tank, you cannot just dive in there and fix everything. You can only make changes from the outside of that tank. This is what we do with your planet Earth. This is what we have been doing since the formation of Earth. While we have been monitoring life on your planet, we have noticed the intelligence of the human being has reached a level of self-destruction."

"That is not a total loss for us, if not for the whole planet destruction is in control of a small minority of your human race."

"It's like putting a young piranha in a non-aggressive fish tank, and the most would happen is a couple fins of the other fish would have nibbles on them. Now when the piranha is grown fully in that fish tank, it will eat every fish left in the tank, resulting in total tank destruction."

"Dear chosen ones, we do not want our fish tank destroyed by a few piranhas, namely being your leaders with their fingers on the nuclear triggers. If you all look ahead out the glass dome you will notice your planet ahead."

Maurice looks at the alien and tele-communicates, "That is not our planet ahead with all those ghostly circles going from ground to atmosphere and back."

All the astronauts were astonished at what they were seeing.

The Soulfurian tele-communicated to them, "We filtered our glass dome with a chemical so all of you can view your planet, as we see it through our eyes. Those ghostly circles as you describe are Starsouls."

"There are billions of them, constantly traveling from ground to your atmosphere and vice versa."

You see when the big bang happened, it formed galaxies, with millions of stars in them. Each star emits Starsouls out to the planets in the solar system. The planets with the right atmospheric conditions collect all the Starsouls. A combined positive and negative cosmic energy. This energy can change in every Starsoul, with more positive or negative energy through the life of the Starsoul. The life of a Starsoul is infinite until the Starsoul has a bigger negative composition, which makes it no longer cosmically balanced, and falls victim to the Star in that solar system."

"Any Star or planet's atmosphere will feed off any other Star's Starsouls.

Once an atmosphere intake a Starsoul from another Star's planet's atmosphere, it will emit them a new Starsouls into its planet's atmosphere. That was an early breakthrough we discovered in our Starsoul experimentations, millions of years back."

What that means is, every one of you has a Starsoul that energizes your body. It is in the middle of your brain. It energizes your thoughts, your speech, your body movements, your heart and your brain."

"Your eyes are the eyes of your Starsoul. When you look into someone's eyes, you're looking at their Starsoul. It is the driving force behind everything you do. It is an inexhaustible supply of energy for your body. Everything living in your solar system has a Starsoul. The only things that do not have Starsouls, are things that are not living. For an object to move it needs energy."

"Your Starsoul is that source of energy for the life of your physical body. You are your Starsoul, and your Starsoul resides in your body for a short time, and then you leave your body to join all the rest of the Starsouls, that energize your atmosphere, then one day to return, and energize another body of your Starsoul type."

"Your Starsoul lives forever, it has so much energy, it wears out its body that it occupies, and takes on a new one until that one dies, and moves onto the next, and so on, and so on. You, and your fellow humans can only witness Starsouls in action in your atmosphere at nighttime, in the northern and southern hemispheres. Your humans refer to these Starsouls as the Northern and Southern lights. This is the time when Starsouls are not busy energizing, and moving the atmosphere, but are at rest, and dance under the moon's glow."

"When a balanced Starsoul is not occupying a physical body, it is traveling the atmosphere in perfect freedom, and your physical bodies may perish but your Starsoul will live on unless it becomes corrupt, and imbalanced with more negative energy."

"Once that happens it will be extinguish by its Star. Once a Starsoul has left a physical body and is introduced into the atmosphere it may change to a different size Starsoul and take on a different form of the body it previously occupied."

"Example: once the normal house fly Starsoul left its body it came back into existence as a bigger force to fuel a horsefly body. Same form of creature but much bigger, and more advanced in time."

"The Starsouls, once reintroduced to the atmosphere can become cosmically bigger, and more advanced in cosmic force to accommodate the new creature on reentry."

"Example: the little sparrow Starsoul can become infused to a Bald Eagle Starsoul, staying along the same type of creature's cosmic energy.

"While in atmospheric life, to be reintroduced to a newborn eagle, and power it to become a fully-grown Bald Eagle."

"Remember a Starsoul is the driving force behind every growth of the body, and the direction the body takes in forming. Look down at your planet now and see the Starsouls rising from the planet."

"That equals all the living things dying and freeing the Starsouls to join the atmosphere until reentry."

"You see the combination of all the billions of billions Starsouls energies, actually powers the atmosphere that circles your planet. They are very much the energy that moves the Gulf Stream, powers the wind, and drives the waves in your oceans."

"Do you notice the millions of Starsouls traveling up past the atmosphere into space, all the way to your Sun? These are dominate with negative cosmic energy and headed for extinguishing. You see every Star needs a balance of Starsouls being pulled in as it puts out.

"Every negative Starsoul burns as fuel for the star for a thousand of your years, and then when the Starsoul is burned and turned to ash dust, the Star will exhaust the dust into space with its solar flares".

"You see when your human being bodies die with balanced or positive Starsouls, your body perishes, and your Starsoul rises to the clouds and atmosphere."

"But when your body dies with negative cosmic Starsoul energy, it goes straight to your Sun for extinguishing."

"You can equate the beautiful Sun, which is the thriving source of life, that you wake up to every day is actually your Hell, and the atmosphere and clouds would equal your Heavens. Though all your religions are all correct in their teachings, and we don't want to be your God's, what I am teaching you about Starsouls, you can find the soul taught in most religions interpreted in various forms."

"The truth of Starsouls has yet to be taught. This truth is infused into every human being through our teaching over mankind's existence, as we will show you in time."

"Do you see the moon that circles your Earth? That is a magnet for extinguished Starsoul dust that your Sun's rays emit."

"The burnt dust bounces off your positive atmosphere, and is scooped up on your moon, where it rest. That would make you're your moon full of cosmic negative energy, pulling on the positive cosmic energy in your atmosphere, that moves your oceans, causing your high and low tides on your shores. Are there questions?" The Soulfurian asked in his tele-communication. The Russian astronaut looks at the alien and tele-communicates, "How do Starsouls reenter as life on the Earth after death?"

The Alien looks back at the Russian and tele-communicates, "You see when Starsouls are roaming the clouds, they cling to the rain drops and snowflakes, and travel freely in the air. They are easily breathed in or fall onto fertile females. The female absorbs the Starsoul, and when the male and female fertilize the egg, it resides in the newborn egg developing, and becomes the newborns driving force of life."

"A newborn can have all the physical characteristics of the male and female, but its Starsoul is a one of a kind, unlike the male or female parents."

Eve tele-communicates to the Spangel, "So it's not a myth that more babies are born during snowstorms."

The Canadian astronaut looks at Spangel and tele-communicates, "What kind of things during a human lifetime can a human do to change the balance, of cosmic positive energy in their Starsoul?"

The Spangel looks back at the Canadian astronaut and tele-communicates, "A Starsouls positive and negative balance, can become unbalanced during the bodies life, because of the way the body lived in its lifetime."

"When the body digests certain chemicals, it can throw the Starsoul into a negative state, making the body prone to do negative things."

"Your Starsoul is doing your thinking for you, so if you are thinking negative or evil then most likely your Starsoul is in a negative cosmic state."

"Your Starsoul can balance itself through better lifetime decision making. So as long as your Starsoul is balanced or in a positive state when your body perishes, your Starsoul will roam the atmosphere."

"Once again, as you all see with your eyes, the unlimited forces of Starsouls created by a Solar Star, is limited to that Stars makeup. Different Stars put out different Starsouls, and next we will show you how we are the keepers of Starsouls."

'A lot of the Starsouls in your atmosphere were implanted by us from different Stars, in different Solar system planet's atmospheres. Way back in your time, four point five billion years ago your Planet Earth was formed in your solar system."

"About three point eight billion years ago, the Earth was cool enough to form rocks, while these billions of cyanobacteria and organism Starsouls, were still driving the atmosphere."

"It wasn't till two point three billion years ago that the oxygen levels rose, and not till five hundred seventy million years ago that those Starsouls took form in the oceans, forming insects and fish, and plants on your planet. Your Star at that time, put hard-shell mollusks, vertebrates, fish, spiders, scorpions, and plant Starsouls into you Earth's atmosphere."

"That would cover the explosion in your planets Cambrian Period, your planets Paleozoic Era, your planets Ordovician Period, your planets Silurian Period, and your planets Devonian Period."

"These were and are all the Starsouls that your Star or Sun produced at that time. The rest of the history of your planet was caused by us. We worked very hard, and invested millions of years building your world, and we will show you soon, how we intend to keep it growing," tele-communicated by the Spangel.

"I will go back down to level two to help the crew guide our spaceship back to Soulfuria. I want all of you to stay here and discuss my teachings and enjoy the view as we go through a black hole, to get back to our planet for refueling. "We will make a quick stop then carry on my teachings for you to pass on to your human race."

Just then, the Spangel disappeared down through the floor, and left the astronauts alone. Zhang the

Chinese astronaut tele-communicated to the rest, "I am starting to be a believer in the teachings of the Spangel."

Haruto the Japanese astronaut tele-communicated, "Look at us speaking in telepathy, looking at Starsouls in action, traveling through galaxies faster than anything man can make. How can I not believe?"

Jeremiah the American astronaut tele-communicated, "Look reincarnation of one's soul is in my religion, and alien influence and visitation are familiar in Hinduism, maybe this is what my beliefs are adding up to. I'm not totally sure yet."

Eve tele-communicated, "Well it looks like they are not bringing us back to Earth, unless we are prophesying their teachings. So, let's keep an open mind, and let them totally convince us without a doubt. Their off to a good start, I would conclude so far."

Axel the German astronaut tele-communicated, "Did you see how he compared our planet to their fish tank, and he was leading to Starsoul manipulation from one Star to another, these aliens are something else!"

"Yea," Adam tele-communicated, "He kept saying or leading to, that they were in control of life on our planet through these Starsouls. That's some heavy shit man."

Maurice tele-communicated, "Obviously they have been nothing but great host to us. They are teaching us things we never heard of. The reasoning behind it all is, I really think they are concerned that our countries and leaders will ruin our world."

"These Space angels are here to show us the way to world peace."

"So, let's enjoy the ride, take in knowledge, and go back and lead our world in the right direction."

Dmitry, Charles, Jacques, and Alexandre all agreed with Maurice. They all just took a seat and sat back staring at the stars, as they were whizzing through the vast reaches of space. They were discovering galaxies, and planets they never dreamt of seeing. It was quite a show.

They all were quite at awe of what was happening, and where they were going. The general feeling was they were eager to see this planet Soulfuria.

Meanwhile back on planet Earth, it's been a week since the astronauts were taken, and things were calming down, with only a few mentions of the incident in the news.

There have been no warnings set off, so the general feeling of the public was, the aliens were not coming back.

The country's militaries were busy in the skies. There were a couple incidents of clashes between some country's air forces, over territory air space, also in the oceans with the country's naval forces, with violations of territorial waters. It seemed the old tensions between the countries were rearing their ugly heads again.

On the political front there were different factions taking over in the Middle East, once the U.S. military pulled out, unbalancing democracy they were keeping in check.

On the Eastern front there were military clashes between India and Pakistan.

It unfolded a world problem bigger than they had, before they implemented the worldwide truce between countries in the name of peace.

"Let's listen into the Presidential Address this evening," announced the media commentator in Boston.

"Good evening ladies and gentlemen, I am here to inform you of the alien crises."

"I know you have heard all the negative things that been happening with all the country's militaries, and I'm here to tell you, whenever you let the boy's play with their toys, there's going to be a little roughhouse here and there. I am not concerned about that, and neither are my constituents."

"Let's talk about real developments that our intelligence department has been relaying. Just yesterday we received a ping from one of our astronauts GPS homing devices, in the astronaut's spacesuits."

"This is a ray of hope that the aliens are still around, and hopefully our astronauts are ok. Now I know this was just a ping for about two hours, and then it was gone." That tells me the aliens did comeback for some reason, and we are trying to figure why."

"We have had no new contact with these aliens, and neither has our international space station."

"Because of these events we are keeping our guard up, and I want to renew our need for peace between countries. We have implemented our early warning systems. So, I will say goodnight to all. May you have sweet dreams knowing that all the wonderful people in our military are at home protecting you."

"Soulfuria"

"Look at that," tele-communicated Eve. "What," tele-communicated the French astronaut? "That, right in front of us, there is no stars or nothing at all," communicated Eve.

"That looks like a black hole," tele-communicated Adam. Just as they were about to enter the black hole, everyone heard the spaceship's engines shut down. The ship went in. They all looked around and could see nothing. It was dead silent and pitch black. The only light was coming from their transporters.

Then all at once, there was a long popping sound, like a cork from a wine bottle. Then a giant suction sound, and then one more pop. The next thing you know the lights came back on. The spaceships engines were running again, and they looked out the window to see the black hole behind them.

Just then the disc at the center of the floor opened, and the bluish gas filled tube rose to their level, with the Soulfurian alien in it.

"Well my chosen ones, have you had a discussion about my teachings?" The Alien Soulfurian tele-communicated.

Maurice tele-communicated back, "Why yes, and most agree although most are not

completely convinced about Soulfurians totally running our world."

"Well, I really didn't expect you all to jump on board with just two sessions under your belt. But as sure as we just went through a black hole, you will all come to understand the one truth, and you will all graduate as my human leaders, and carry out our word to your kind."

"You see if your people don't realize how close they are to extinction, and they don't realize that we as Soulfurians could come by your planet, and put you out of your misery, then the later of the two will happen. We will not let the human race that we started on planet Earth, take it upon themselves to ruin what we have been building for millions of years."

Adam looked at the Alien and tele-communicated, "With all due respect to your claim you put man on our planet.

Earlier you claimed not to be our Gods, but now you say you put us on planet Earth. Which is it?"

The rest of the crew looked on wide eyed for the alien's response.

"Yes, you are correct young human, the first humans were put on Earth by us, and you are also correct that we are not Gods. Let's get this straight and not confuse this again."

"Your questions are valid under the state of the unenlightened. I am here to enlighten you and educate you. We are once again keepers of the universes. We are your universe police force. And we see violations against life in general on one of our planets, and we intend to stop it by educating you."

"Your evolution may show how man evolved on your planet, but it doesn't show how we put the first Primates on Earth, and Primate Starsouls in Earth's atmosphere."

"You see your great books don't say how The Great Apes were created. Follow your evolution trail from the first man, and how he evolved from the Ape."

"We will show you the Ape evolved from one of the Hominids we put on Earth, or the Hominids Starsouls we put in Earth's atmosphere. All we know until four hundred and seventeen million years ago, your Earth was nothing but a giant ant farm, with plants just growing on land, and giant insects ruling your world."

"The plant, insect and sea life were from your Suns Starsouls. There you have insects walking your planet, and because at the time the atmosphere was real thick, with twenty percent more oxygen than today. That allowed them to grow to be giant."

"What in the world," tele-communicated by Eve.

Everyone took their attention off the alien Soulfurian, and looked outside the dome, and saw this giant blue green planet they were getting close to. This planet was so big it was twice as big as planet Saturn back home. It was the biggest planet they ever saw.

Jeremiah looked at the Spangel, and tele-communicated to him, "Why can't our telescopes spot this big giant from Earth?"

The Spangel tele-communicated back, "Remember that black hole we went through? Well, we traveled one million light years in that short time. So, you can imagine how much older our civilization is compared to yours."

Just then the whole spaceship was engulfed in bluish green and blue light from the alien atmosphere.

They noticed through the chemical treated glass dome there were ghostly circular bodies flowing, from the planet to its atmosphere and back.

The French astronaut tele-communicated, "They must be Soulfurian Starsouls."

"Yes, it is true," tele-communicated by the Sulfurian Spangel. This is one of many Starsouls I will show you, as soon as our ship is refueled."

"Now when we dock, you all will be allowed to visit our planet. You will need to put on your flight suits, and then dress into your space walking suits."

"You will need your oxygen supply because our atmosphere is composed of Nitrogen gas only."

"You can find planets in your own solar system with atmospheres that contain Nitrogen. Not in the concentrations of ours. Anyway, while we are refueling, you can visit our city of Gaurdonia."

"We call it that because everyone in this city guards, protects, and transports Starsouls to galaxies all over the cosmos."

"Our planet's core is magnetic, but because of the size it's not that powerful."

"Not as powerful as your Earth's gravity."

"We wear lightweight magnets on the soles of our feet. We are fitted for them when we are young. It keeps us stable when traveling. You will bounce up and down like you are on your moon. Its ok, you will not fly away."

"Your weighted metal soles in your space suits will keep you grounded." Then there was a slight bump from the floor as the spaceship landed.

The astronaut crew was instructed to go to their quarters, and get dressed in their flight suits, and transport down to the first level where the Soulfurian crew will hand them their Space suits, equipped with oxygen tanks.

After about thirty minutes, the International Space Walk for Peace team was back in action. The Canadian astronaut tele-communicated, "I thought I would never see us in these suits again."

Maurice looked at him and tele-communicated, "Let's wear them proudly and enter this new frontier on a mission for all mankind."

Adam looked at Maurice and tele-communicated, "You're starting to sound like John Wayne over there Island Man."

The crew went out the exit ramp to the planet surface. They were in awe once again; at the landscape they saw once they bounced down the ramp.

It was a barren moonscape with a light sandy surface, with the bluish green skyline, it was an awesome sight. Adam spoke in his space suit walkie talkie, "This looks like the first time I visited New York City wearing blue shades." There were these little two seat alien flying vehicles everywhere overhead, about thirty feet in the air. It seems nothing on the planet was any higher than that.

Only a small magnetism was on the plane, so anything with an engine could become airborne.

The American astronauts were cut off from the other astronauts, as far as communication. So, unless they were looking at each other in the space helmets, they could not communicate through telepathy.

The five American astronauts had working walkie- talkies in their helmets. Jeremiah said, "Hell it's great to speak with our voices again, I thought I lost mine."

Eve said, "Look at those flying cars above, they don't make a sound, and there's no by-product coming from the cars."

Maurice replies, "Remember these aliens are millions of years ahead of us in technology, so those cars could be running on nuclear fusion or something like that."

A crowd of alien Soulfurians surrounded the twelve astronauts, as they were hopping without gravity to what looked like an airplane hangar cutout the side of a mountain.

It was weird that the aliens or Soulfurians had skin that resembled human beings.

Also, there were different shades of skin on these Soulfurians like there is on Earth, with some having dark shades, and some having reddish shades also black, brown and yellow shades. Kind of the same shades the astronauts were.

Jeremiah looked back and noticed the alien crew refueling the spaceship. They were pulling six-foot-long stainless-steel tubes that were about twelve inches in diameter out of the side of the spaceship and replacing them with new ones. They looked like giant nuclear fuel rods.

"So, Maurice, once again you're right, it looks as if they have a nuclear reactor powering the spaceship," said Jeremiah.

Once they arrived inside the building in the mountain Adam says, "Boy when we got off the spaceship it looked pretty desolate outside, but once in here it looks like they're a million years ahead of us in technology."

There were computers, three-dimensional video screens, and tram cars riding on air. It looked like Grand Central Station with an alien twist.

This place was humongous. As the whole astronaut crew came in, the lead alien Soulfurian directed the crew to a resting area and told them to stay there until refueling was complete, also it was time to go. So all the astronauts took their seats, and watched this planet of aliens going in every direction in this mountain. Eve said, "Look at what a lot of these Soulfurians are carrying"

"Yeah, right, it looks like there importing and exporting air or something," said Malone.

The Soulfurians were carrying cylindrical tubes that looked like nothing was in them. They were all puzzled why they were doing this.

The twelve astronauts were a special attraction in the Soulfurian metropolis, drawing curious crowds around them.

They were funny looking to the on looking Soulfurians, with their giant round space helmet heads. As soon as one of the astronauts would turn to look at the aliens, the whole bunch of them would scatter in fear of the humans. Adam would turn really fast and go, "boo", to scare the Soulfurians away. Eve would fire back to Adam, "Stop that, that's not nice Adam!"

The Soulfurian aliens were a non-violent passive species. It seemed they all had a job to do, transporting these empty cylinders in and out of the mountainous warehouse.

The leader Soulfurian came walking over to the humans, and tele-communicated to them to go with him to a doorway on the side corridor. When he walked up to the door, it automatically opened.

Inside the room were walls with dispenser machines, and a giant 3D video screen above them. These screens were just floating in the air with nothing attached to them.

The Soulfurian tele-communicated to the twelve, "to look at the video screens, and telepath your wishes for food and drink, and wish enough to last about a week, also think of different meals snacks, and drinks."

They all found screens to look at. As they were concentrating, food rations appeared on the tables in front out of thin air. They were just like military rations the astronauts were familiar with, only with alien packaging. They were all instructed to grab a carry bag for their food supply and head out the corridor to the area where they arrived. All the astronauts were bouncing up and down in the little gravity mountain floor.

They were shuffling to get their bags and get out of there. When they came out of the room, the giant 3D video screen was on now.

In the main area where they entered, Soulfurian aliens on the screen directed the ones on the ground floor to go to different colored spheres on the screen. They were showing those tubular canisters with nothing in them.

The Chinese astronaut Zhang looked at the Soulfurian leader and tele-communicated, "Why are all your Soulfurians carrying those empty canisters in and out of here?"

"Also, why is that Soulfurian up on the screen directing them to take the canisters to those different color spheres?" The Leader Soulfurian stepped back and motioned all the astronauts to line up against the wall, so he has all their attention.

He looks at them all from left to right and tele-communicates, "We are the keepers of the universes.

From the time we are young till our old age we travel the cosmos. We see dying planets and transform them with life."

"If we see a planet getting out of control with a certain species, we may introduce another species to balance life off. What you see here is our force of ten billion Soulfurians, working nonstop to keep the universes fruitful."

"What they are transporting in those canisters are Starsouls. They are all Starsouls from all galaxies, and all planet atmospheres."

"You as humans cannot see Starsouls unless you are looking through our spacecraft windows. We are the only species that can see, capture, contain, transport, and plant Starsouls."

"The purpose of our mission with you, is to teach you the reasoning behind life on your planet, and show you how we formed your planet, and nurtured it to the state it is in today."

"Then when you go back to your planet with this knowledge, you will understand enough to teach your human race."

"You will now bring your bag of rations, and drinks, and head back to the spaceship as the ship is refueled, and ready for a journey."

The crew grabbed their bags and bounced back outside on their way back to the spaceship. Adam radioed to his fellow American astronauts on the way back, "Well, it looks like we are in for one hell of an adventure."

Maurice radioed back, "Yea and it looks like we are going to get one hell of a history lesson."

Eve radioed back, "If what he says is true, and we see it with our own eyes, there's no book or story going to make me think otherwise." Adam chirped back in his "John Wayne" voice, "Well he can talk the talk, but can he walk the walk?"

"The Cosmos"

The crew was inside the spaceship finishing putting their rations away in their quarters, then the buzzer once again sounded. The twelve astronauts knew what that meant. They made their way to their transporters, in their blue jumpsuits to travel up to the sky view deck and settled themselves in the seats on that level.

The spaceship was pulling away from the bluish green planet. It seemed forever because of its size. The astronauts can once again see the Soulfurian Starsouls moving their blue green atmosphere, flowing freely around their planet. The most peaceful event they ever laid their eyes on.

"Onto the cosmos we go," tele-communicated by the Soulfurian Leader to his commanding crew. Now they were away from Soulfuria, and they could see the solar system it was in. There were no other giant planets rotating around their Star. The ship was moving now at warp speed away into the cosmos.

The British astronaut Charles tele-communicated to the Spangel, "Where are we off to now chap?"

The alien responded to the Brit, "My chosen one, you may call me the leader, Spangel, Soulfurian or enlightened one, but please don't refer to me as chap. Now where did I leave off in our last session, better yet can anyone tell me what you have learned already?" 'Can we recap?"

Eve started off by tele-communicating, "The reason you took us, was to make us your prophets to spread your teachings to our people."

"Very good" tele-communicated the Spangel.

The Russian, Dmitri tele-communicated next, "When you captured us you opened a part of our brain that humans didn't develop yet, so we are able to communicate with each other, and you through telepathy."

"Yes indeed," tele-communicated the Spangel," "Anyone else?"

The American Jeremiah tele-communicated, "The reason you are upset with our human race, is the fact that we developed as a society to the point of self-destruction, and then you compared our world to being your fishbowl. The same fishbowl you worked millions of years to build, and you don't want to see us ruin it."

"That is right, that is the main reason you are here, but there's one more thing I would like one of you to tell me."

"Starsouls" tele-communicated by the German named Axel. "You and your species can see something no other species can see. That makes you the keepers of the very thing, in all living things, their Starsouls. Galaxies have solar systems who have Stars, that put out little burst of energy called Starsouls. The planet in the solar system with the right conditions, collects the entire Star's Starsouls."

"These Starsouls are responsible for energizing everything living and moving on the planet."

"The only way a Starsoul can be extinguished, is to become cosmically unbalanced, with a negativity greater than positivity. Then it becomes so light, it floats up and gets reclaimed by its Star for Star fuel. "

"Yes," was tele-communicated by Zhang the Chinese astronaut. Your Starsoul can become negative by your lifestyle, and decisions during your lifetime. As long as you live your life good enough to balance your Starsoul's cosmic balance, your Starsoul will live another lifetime. So, there is hope for eternal salvation."

The Spangel tele-communicated, "All of you are good learners, but what I need to show you, is that we are responsible for evolving your world, and what steps we took to accomplish that, in millions of your years' time."

"Where I left off in your last session, was with your Star or Sun. When your planet was formed, it only put out Starsouls of organisms, plants, insects, and sea life in many forms."

"It was a lush green world with a thick atmosphere, loaded with these billions of sea life, and plant Starsouls."

"You're Devonian Period of fish in the water, plants, and insects, were the only things traveling all around your planet. Like the pollen travels in the summertime, like a fog in the morning, like a breeze when it blows on your face. Starsouls of lush green forest formed in Earth's atmosphere, about three hundred million years ago. When all your planet's landmasses came together to form what you humans call Pangea."

"It took about a million years for green plant seeds to mix with green forest Starsouls, and form Coal forming forest all over Pangea. About forty million years later the forest were growing out of control, the planet was overrun by insects, and greenery, kind of like algae growing all over your fish tank."

We needed to do something, to keep all the greenery and insects at bay on Pangea. This was a time when we started to transfer Starsouls."

"We will be coming up on the Carnherbivorous galaxy, where we first obtained Starsouls of the first creatures that we introduced to Earth's atmosphere."

"Just sit back and enjoy the cosmos as we near our first stop." Just then the Spangel with his blue-green gas infused tube lowered into the center room floor and descended to the second level.

"Are you kidding me?" Adam telecommunicated, "I know these cats are old, but three hundred fifty million years ago they were trimming our trees?"

Zhang tele-communicates, "That period of time is older than any book written by man."

Axel telecommunicates, "Checkout how they turned green plants into lush green forest."

The French astronaut Jacques tele-communicated to the group, "Remember our Sun formed the Starsouls of all the greenery, sea life and insects on our planet, not the Soulfurians."

Eve tele-communicated, "I can't wait to see the first creatures they mixed in our atmosphere."

So while the astronauts were waiting to enter the Carnherbivorous galaxy. Things were brewing back at home.

Back home on Planet Earth, it has been six months now since the tragedy in space. Most people are going on with their daily lives, with little mention on the news of any updates on the missing astronauts.

The leaders of the different countries are pointing fingers at each other over the space tragedy, and how each other's countries should have prevented the crisis from happening. On the military front, most nations have all their military at home, protecting their borders and skies.

"From the desk of WPRT here in Kansas City, "this is reporter Russell Prinkton, bringing you the Six o'clock News. The big story tonight is The Russian Prime Minister Igor Vakhrov was requesting an internal investigation, two days ago at the United Nations general assembly.

He was accusing the United States of organizing the Space Walk for Peace, and not spending the money allocated for defense and safety for the astronauts and keeping the funds to finance another space mission for the United States.

The spokesperson from Washington called the Russian Prime minister, "ludicrous", and called his allegations "preposterous." This outraged the Prime minister as he walked up and left the general assembly meeting.

The United Nations passed a resolution to form an international space defense system. We are waiting for the President to make his "State of the Union Address," to reveal the details.

"Let's go now to the Presidential Address live in Washington, as we wait for the President to speak.

"Good evening fellow Americans. I am grateful to speak to you tonight. Tonight marks the six month anniversary of "The International Space Walk for Peace."

"A walk unique in the sense, for our twelve international astronauts."

"They have trained in every aspect of space flight, only to come across something they could never be ready for in their wildest dreams. It was a tragic event that will burn in our minds forever, and an awakening for the future generations of the human race."

"So I have met with all of my cabinet, and they have met with our friends in the United Nations, to come up with a plan to protect and defend all astronauts visiting the International Space Station, and all of Space. This plan will protect against any future alien attack in our Earth's orbit."

"In the next five years, with the help of all our neighboring countries, we will be building an "International Military Defense Space Station right alongside the I.S.S."

"We will incorporate all the latest missile and space weaponry. We will have an early radar warning system loaded aboard the defense space station."

"Detail of this development, will be available in press releases to the media."

"As you know, it has been six months since the tragedy, and we have not given up hope on our astronauts return. We are watching the skies as the daily public is conducting their daily business. There have been no updates on the situation, and as soon as they come, we will inform the public. I will take some questions on recent developing matters. "

"Young lady in the front row, you can go first."
"Hello, Mr. President, this is Kelly Heart from WHDS

from Denver, I want to ask you, what can be going through the minds of those astronauts, if they are still alive. They must feel they are in a virtual nightmare."

"Good question Ms. Heart, I know those proud men and woman are mind strong through this ordeal, and I believe they are doing everything they need to survive. Remember now they are people of the military that have been trained in being prisoners of war, and I know this is a new war, so to speak. I believe they are united and strong."

"Next question please, you over there in the gray blazer." "Hello Mr. President, I am Robert Harmer the Third, from WYYL in Tuscan Arizona, with a question on the latest news report, about the accusations the Russian Prime minister made against the United States, about funds for defense. Also, does that hurt relations with them in terms of a joint relationship with this crisis?"

"A two part answer I believe you need there Mr. Harmer." "First let me start out by saying we have a great relationship with the Russian federation."

"Our fellow American astronauts are with a Russian cosmonaut as we speak, and if they only knew we were questioning our solidarity down here they would be laughing. Yes, the Prime minister had a bad day at the general assembly, but cooler heads had revealed."

"You see, we are just scratching our heads how we were so blind to all the dangers, and possibilities we faced venturing space."

"When you are in that position, you start grabbing at straws, and I think that was the case the other day. Things get a little twisted out of context, as the story gets passed down from person to person."

"No matter whom it is, each person has to add their own twist to the story, and when it finally reaches you, the story has arms and legs, and a big hairy back, if you know what I mean."

"I called the Russian Prime minister yesterday, and I assure you things are sound between us."

"I will have to run now; I will return with better news next time, I hope. Good night America, just remember we are watching the skies for you."

Meanwhile, the astronauts are doing various things aboard the Soulfurian spaceship. The Russian is napping in bed, while the French and English men are chatting in telepathy on the second level.

The Chinese astronaut is meditating in his quarters. The German and Japanese astronauts are laughing over in the corner on the observation deck.

The Canadian and the five Americans are watching the galaxy, as they are all traveling at the speed of light.

"Could you imagine how far we are from home?" tele-communicates Eve, as she stares out the alien observation window.

Adam replies with his "John Wayne" impression, "You're a long way from Kansas Dorothy."

Maurice communicates, "Look ahead, it looks like we are coming up on a galaxy with a few planets."

" I wonder if this is where they are taking us." Jeremiah communicates, "Yea, those planets look a lot like Earth, I wonder what's on those planets."

"Malone communicates, "Well, if you go by what the Soulfurian was saying, it must be some kind of plant eater."

Just then the buzzer sounded, that meant for all the astronauts to join the five Americans, and the Canadian for the next Soulfurian intelligence meeting.

The Russian came from his quarters, and transported up, then the French, and English astronaut came up.

Then the Chinese astronaut came from his meditation and joined the rest on the observation level.

Just then the gold circle in the middle of the room opened, and the Soulfurian rose up in his blue-green gas infused tube, until it came to rest on the third level.

"Carnherbivorous Galaxy"

"Welcome back to our intelligence sessions my chosen ones." The Soulfurian tele-communicated, as he panned his head at the astronauts around the room. "As you look out the glass dome, can you describe what you see?"

The Chinese astronaut looks at the Spangel and tele-communicates, "I see a vast solar system with multiple blue sphere planets that look a lot like our planet Earth." "Yes" tele-communicates the German. "They are all in a straight line, and all the same distance from its star."

"You are both correct, tele-communicated the Soulfurian. They are a lot like your blue planet, or maybe back in the early days of your planet."

"They are about ninety-three million miles from its Star, almost the same distance your planet is from your star. As we get closer, we will see how dense the planet's atmosphere is. It is really thick on all four upcoming planets. We call this the Carnherbivorous Galaxy. And the first planet we will visit in this solar system is called, "Reptilia."

As the spaceship gets closer and penetrates Reptilia's atmosphere, the astronauts are astonished by what they see.

Eve looks out the glass, and tele-communicates, "There are those Starsouls again, these ones are green and brown."

The astronauts can get an up-close view of the billions of reptile Starsouls streaming its atmosphere.

"Wow, this atmosphere is dense, and there are billions of these things traveling in all directions," tele-communicated Axel, the German astronaut.

As the ship lowered to land, the astronauts looked outside, and there was a terrestrial world around them. There were forest, streams, and reptiles everywhere on the ground. Reptiles and more reptiles roamed the planet. The astronauts could not believe their eyes. "The spaceship has landed," tele-communicated the Soulfurian.

"Although I, or any of my crew cannot go outside, you are all welcome to step outside, walk and observe the reptilian creatures."

The British astronaut tele-communicated, "Are you kidding me?"

"No," tele-communicated the Soulfurian.

"The planet is rich with oxygen, and you don't need your spacesuits. Now all of you go outside, and spend a little time observing the first creatures we put on your planet three hundred forty million years ago."

The astronauts in their blue jumpsuits went to their transporters and took them down to the first level. There was a stairwell to the outside ground. They all started down. Once they reached the ground, they were all astonished they were standing, and breathing on another planet.

"This is just too real," says Adam.

"Yea, it's like we're in the South American rainforest," says Maurice.

"Look at all the reptiles around us," says Jeremiah.

"It looks like we are the visitors in their world. The world of lizards and turtles, and a lot of reptiles we never saw before," said Malone.

Axel the German astronaut came back from a little stroll.

He looked at the Americans and tele-communicated, "I would not advise walking near the river's edge over there, it's full of alligators, crocodiles and snakes."

It was quite warm on the planet where the astronauts were located. It was somewhere in the ninety-degree range.

There was lush forest with volcanoes in the distance. There were swamps, and valleys. It seemed like they were in a rainforest back at home.

"This place is starting to creep me out," says Eve. "Let's go back inside the spaceship."

"I don't like them wormy lizards over there, and those caimans over there by the swamp."

"So, these were the first creatures the Soulfurians claim to put on our planet. I would like to see the Soulfurian explain how they did this myself," tele-communicated Jacques, the French astronaut.

"Ok, let's head back, we saw enough of this reptilian paradise. I would like to know the names of some here."

"They don't look familiar on our planet," tele-communicated by Dmitri, the Russian astronaut.

So the crew headed back to the spaceship. They didn't stay long in that environment. There could have been lurking dangers they did not want to come across. They were on one hand amazed, and shocked that another world with oxygen breathing creatures could exist.

Then instinctively harboring in the back of their minds, the aliens could take off, and leave their butts there to fend in the wild.

They were eager to hear how the Soulfurians put all these creatures in their world three hundred million years ago.

The twelve astronauts one by one made their way into the spaceship getting into their transporters and meeting up on the third level where the Soulfurian was waiting in his glass enclosed tube. The spaceship is docked on the planet of reptiles.

When the astronauts look from the third level glass, they have a better 360-degree view of the world they are on, and with the special dome glass, they also can see the Starsouls, the Soulfurian is teaching about.

The Soulfurian alien pans his head from left to right at the astronauts and tele-communicates, "Well,

well my chosen ones, did you all get a nice firsthand encounter of the reptiles here on this planet?"

"Yes, we did," tele-communicated Zhang, the Chinese Astronaut.

"Now, is this where you are going to link these creatures with our planet's evolution?"

"Yes indeed," tele-communicates the Soulfurian. "This is the beginning to where I link our control of all your planets evolution."

"We took your world from a giant greenhouse full of insects, and land crawling vertebrae that evolved from the sea, to the self-mutilating society it has evolved to today."

"About three hundred fifteen million years ago, Pangea was crawling with amphibians, insects, and because the atmosphere was still rich and thick like the one here, some of those insects grew to be giant. We were not satisfied with developing Planet Earth. We knew it was far greater of supporting multiple species of life. More than what your star could provide."

"That is where we started growing our little fish tank, so to speak."

We traveled to this Galaxy and came across this planet and saw the tens of thousands of reptile species here. We collected Starsouls from this atmosphere and transported them to plant them into your Earth's atmosphere. The reptile Starsouls would travel throughout Earth's atmosphere for fifteen million years."

"Starsouls would seek out fertile female amphibians like tetrapod that evolved the first amphibians, capable of dwelling both in the water and on the land, in some cases male amphibian and attaching to their eggs. It took fifteen million years for this transformation to work. To have those amphibians transform, and flourish into ten thousand species of reptiles roaming your planet Earth."

"What were some of those reptiles we saw today on this planet?" Charles the British astronaut tele-communicated to the Soulfurian.

The Soulfurian tele-communicated back to the Brit with, "They are various species of original reptiles and original Starsouls we transported, which would equal the ancestors of the reptiles you see on your planet today."

"So, let me get this straight," tele-communicated by Haruto, the Japanese astronaut. "Evolution started on our planet Earth only to the point of sea life and green vegetation?"

"Then from that point on, you the space angels' guardians of Starsouls, the ultimate controllers of life on our planet, are going to tell us you are not Gods?"

"What you mean by the word God might not mean the same for your neighbor as it does to you."

"We Soulfurians, also believe there is a God. An entity that was worthy of being a God would have the power to create the Big Bang, create the stars, create the galaxies, create Starsouls and life as a whole. We as Soulfurians believe all life derives from electrical cosmic energy mixed with gas, minerals and compounds."

"We were created by the same energy producing God as you were many billions of years before you."

"That in itself gives us the knowledge, wisdom, and technology to be the keepers of the galaxies, and Starsouls, not the creators. With the responsibility of manipulating life on planets and solar systems, it is purely biological and science. We take it very seriously."

"When your human technologies advanced to the point of stem cell research to grow body parts and test tube babies, would that give you the status of being called God's? I think not, just a prime example of what we do on a bigger scale."

"Our main mission in the galaxies, is to sustain life on planets constantly changing in temperature and mass. Such a change happened on planet Earth fifty million years after we introduced your atmosphere with reptile Starsouls, which led to reptiles roaming on the planet.

The planet's land mass all came together as one land mass. Your humans called it Pangea."

"Well, Pangea eventually dried up from a massive global warming period, to the point one hundred seventy-five million years ago."

"It wiped out ninety-six percent of all life on Planet Earth. This would mark the end of what your humans call the Permian Period, where it was a time of biological dividing lines, where only a minority of species crossed."

"We will break now as I will go to help my crew with taking off from this Reptilian planet and venturing on to the next planet in this Carnherbivorous galaxy."

As the Soulfurian's glass tube lowers into the ground, the astronauts are all gazing out the window, watching the green Starsouls travel throughout the atmosphere, at the same time they are soaking in everything the Space angel had to say.

"This is some for real shit," tele-communicated by Adam. "After all we saw so far, and everything we have learned, I think these cats are for real."

"As true as everything seems now, it's still going to take a lot more than this to convince me," tele-communicated Axel, the German astronaut.

"Well, keep your eyes and ears open, because it looks like we are headed to another one of these blue planets in this Carnherbivorous galaxy's solar system," tele-communicated by Maurice.

"Let's take a vote around the room, how many believe in these Soulfurians, and who they are, although it's everything against what we were taught to believe back on Earth," tele-communicated by Eve.

"Just raise your hand if you believe in their story." As Eve looked around the room, Adam had his hand up with the English, the Brit, Japanese, and Canadian Astronauts.

"Ok, that makes five out of twelve, and they are not going to let us go back to Earth unless we all believe in them, and go back as their prophets," tele-communicated by Eve.

"Well, if we look back since the nineteen forties when our government allegedly captured an alien spacecraft, and aliens that look exactly like these Soulfurians in area fifty-one in Roswell New Mexico, our technology has since exploded.

So there has to be a lot of truth to what the Soulfurian is preaching, and for me that means I am slowly becoming convinced," Zhang, the Chinese astronaut tele-communicates to the crew.

"The Soulfurian has demonstrated that they can capture and transfer these Starsouls by what we saw on Planet Soulfuria, and what we can see through their spaceship windows." "What they are showing us by this telepathy ability, and how he explained the transformation of living things on Earth to this point is pretty convincing."

"Although I would still like to see how he explains the origins of man, and how they provided the technology for man to use. I'm not totally convinced yet, I need to see more," tele-communicated Adam.

Dmitri, the Russian astronaut simply tele-communicated, "I need to see more to be totally convinced, although at this point, I am pretty impressed."

Jacques, the French astronaut tele-communicates to the crew,

"I cannot believe this new way of thinking, unless he can show us how the Soulfurians were involved in every step of human evolution. And for him to do this will be one hell of a ride."

Jeremiah tele-communicates, "I believe in something else. I was brought up that way, and although everything I was taught is based on belief, this

Soulfurian is showing me facts in front of my own eyes. It will take a lot more evidence to change my point of view. Well people, I believe we are pioneers for the human race."

"Already aboard this mission, we have knowledge greater than our people on alien belief."

"We can communicate through telepathy, which means we are the only humans in history capable of doing that, and we are the only humans that have witnessed Starsouls in action. So, I think it is our duty as human beings to seek the truth whatever it may be, and whatever beliefs it may conflict with," tele-communicated by Maurice, the last American astronaut to comment.

When the crew was finished discussing their beliefs in what the Space angel was teaching them, there was a distant planet in the viewing window they were drawing closer to.

"Look over there," Zhang tele-communicated to the others. It was a giant blue planet just Like Earth, but about five times bigger.

"I can't believe we are looking straight at another alien planet Earth," tele-communicated by Malone.

The spaceship is getting real close to the planet now. They are being overshadowed by the giant planet.

. "Look, the atmosphere is full of blue-green Starsouls," tele-communicated by Eve.

"Yes, and look there are giant oceans of water on the planet," tele-communicated by Axel, the German astronaut.

"Look, there are giant animals all over the planet. I can see them on the land masses," tele-communicated by Jeremiah.

Just then the circle in the floor opened up, and then a bluish-green gas filled tube emerged through it and rose to the third level.

"Well, it looks like our teacher is back to give us another lesson," tele-communicated by Adam.

The Soulfurian reached the third level, after helping its crew navigate from Reptilia to the upcoming planet. He slowly pans the room to get all the astronaut's attention, and tele-communicates to them.

"Ok my chosen ones, where did I leave off with you? I believe it was the Permian Period. It was when most of life was eliminated on Planet Earth, two hundred and forty-seven million years ago, after two million years of our reptile inhabitation of Earth."

"You can read from your evolution book on Earth, there was a planet mass extinction, caused by normal planet growing changes in temperatures, and volcanic gases, also land reformation."

"Most of the reptiles that we transported could not handle the extreme temperature changes, so ninety percent of their bodies perished, but their Starsouls recycled in the atmosphere. All the natural marine life that was supplied by your Star was virtually wiped out."

"This was the time we traveled back to the Carnherbivorous galaxy and came upon this second planet in this solar system called Triassica. "This is where you can see an abundance of mammals, and the earliest species of dinosaurs. This was about two hundred fifty million years ago, in what you would call the Mesozoic Era."

"We are going to hover just high enough above the ground to be able to give you a tour of this planet, so you can see what type of creatures we decided to evolve on planet Earth."

"Look to the left over by the rocks and see the first archosaurs and therapsids. They are lizards and mammal-like reptiles. Look over to the right by the tall trees, there is a Plesiosaurus. He is an early plant eating dinosaur. Now as we travel over this ridge, you can see the Herrerasaurus and the Eoraptor. These were the first true dinosaur Starsouls that we could transport."

"Because the Permian Extinction depopulated the world's oceans, the Triassic planet was a good place to extract the Placodus and Nothosaurus for the first time."

"We went to this atmosphere and captured all the Starsouls of the creatures you see here. All the Starsouls of the marine life and fish you see here."

"We transported them to Earth's atmosphere. It took nineteen million years for these Starsouls to mix with all the surviving reptiles on Earth."

"The fertile reptiles would acquire these dinosaur Starsouls. Until, two hundred and thirty one million years ago, the first dinosaurs roamed your planet. The vast Panthalassan Ocean, soon found itself restocked with new species of prehistoric fish. And simple animals like corals and cephalopods."

"We let the first Dinosaurs, and mammals develop on Planet Earth for twenty-two million years. By this time, there were plenty of plant eating smaller dinosaurs, and plenty of sea life in our aquarium called Earth. Once again, I will break to help my crew navigate this spaceship to our next destination. Discuss, and get a bite to eat with your meal rations you received from Planet Soulfuria."

"Reptilia to Triassica"

Just then the Space Angel Soulfurian, lowered his glass tube into the circular cut out in the floor and disappeared.

"I don't know if this is a nightmare or a dream," tele-communicated by the Russian astronaut. "They developed the dinosaurs from transporting their Starsouls to our atmosphere, and then they turned small reptiles into small dinosaurs through Starsoul transformation."

"This is cardinal knowledge for us," tele-communicated by the French astronaut.

"I can't believe what I am seeing, and what I am hearing. It's like everything I was taught to believe was just ripped away to this stark reality," tele-communicated by Eve.

"I'm hungry, I'm just going to my quarters to fix me something to eat," tele-communicated by the German astronaut.

"He calls these Starsouls cosmic energy, but from what he describes by the power they have, they must contain D.N.A, the basic building blocks of life," tele-communicated the Japanese astronaut.

"No, I don't think so, I think it is more like the cosmic energy as he describes. It is the driving force to grow D.N.A. It is cosmic energy from stardust, the very building blocks of everything in this universe," tele-communicated by the Chinese astronaut.

"So, I'm the person who is thinking in my head right now, could be the Starsoul from an early settler in the seventeen hundreds, and also the same Starsoul from one of the very first humans on Earth," tele-communicated by Jeremiah.

"I'm afraid so my friend, from what the Space Angel is teaching us, we are all part of a great system of life made of energy that keeps regenerating over and over."

"It makes the whole concept of dying so comforting, because when our bodies perish, our Starsouls are free to roam the atmosphere to no bounds and re-energize to a newborn body to live another human life in the future," tele-communicated by Maurice.

"Did you ever dream you lived another life at one time? I did, and everyone I know did. I wonder if it is left over memory bits of our Starsouls?" tele-communicated by Adam.

"It seems the whole point of Starsouls is to keep a positive life, and keep evil or negative energy at bay, before the end of your mortal life, or at all times because your mortal life can end at any moment in time," tele-communicated Charles.

"It seems ironic that you do crazy things while you are young and spend the rest of your life doing good things to counter your younger actions, which is what the cosmic Starsoul theory is all about."

It's like we knew it all along," tele-communicated by Malone the American astronaut.

"Now that is food for thought. Let's go get some grub on that note," tele-communicated by the Canadian astronaut.

All the astronauts returned to their transporters, and to their quarters to get a bite to eat. The Soulfurian was with his crew navigating the spaceship away from Triassica into the cosmos. It is now time to see what is transforming back on planet Earth.

"The Alien Scare is Over" The title read on the front page of the New York Gazette. The newscasters were reporting of all countries getting back to business, and redeploying troops overseas, away from their homeland. All military air defenses were on minimum alert, and things were getting back to normal. It has been 8 months without incident, and the Space Station tragedy was eager to be put in the past.

Although for the general world public, it was still fresh in the back of their minds, the whole incident they could still paint in their heads.

They would rather put the alien incident behind them. It was not a good topic for conversation around the dinner table. If you believed in the aliens you were cast an atheist, and a crazy nut, although the whole world witnessed them. "Some things are better left unsaid." It was quoted by one of the leading clergies. The aliens were being the center of punch lines on late night talk shows.

The world was in a state of denial as their busy lives pushed them on their way. Although movies with aliens and new, and old toys of aliens were popping up all over. By now, they are being cast the familiar bad villain. No one saw any of the aliens that took the astronauts, but their imaginations were running wild in the movie studios in Hollywood.

Onto another subject, there was a real hotspot over in Europe, as Russia was looking to take over Ukraine.

They were gearing their military up for a complete takeover.

The U.S. was upset over this move, causing them to threaten the Russian Federation with sanctions, and a possible embargo on goods shipped there.

The U.S President was no longer giving State of the Union speeches on aliens to the American public. Instead giving them updates on the Russian moves. On the other front, China was boosting up their military along with North Korea. They were being observant with the renewed military exercises between the U.S. and Japan, and the US, and South Korea. India and Pakistan were jawing new threats at each other.

It was a complete international military mess. Countries were back to communicating by their military muscle, and not their peaceful negotiations. Things were back to the way they were before the astronaut tragedy crisis. These are the events worrying the Soulfurians. Now we go back to the Soulfurian's spacecraft and see that the astronauts are busy in their quarters.

Suddenly, the astronauts heard the buzzer going off, knowing that meant for them to return to the third level for more education briefings.

As the astronauts were getting themselves to their transporters, the Soulfurian was already up there waiting for them to arrive.

One by one the transporter doors opened up, and the astronauts joined the Soulfurian. They were looking at him in his glass enclosed tube. Once all twelve were present, the Soulfurian scanned his eyes from one side to the other, until he received all their attention. He started by tele-communicating to them, developments unfolding backed on Earth were very upsetting to the Soulfurian community. Once he communicated that, he had all their attention.

He looked at them and tele-communicated, "There have been breaking events back on your planet, proving the handful of piranhas were back at threatening each other again."

"Your world leaders took their minds off your disappearance and went back to their aggressive ways again. This makes us Soulfurians, keepers of the universe very uncomfortable. As long as we have you here, we cannot complete our mission and bring your world to peace and working together united."

"We are playing a high game of stakes here. We are in a race to educate you of our mission and get you back to preach our ways before your world, and our fishbowl go to waste, with unbalanced Starsouls leading your nations."

"Can you tell us what is happening?" tele-communicated by Zhang, the Chinese astronaut.

"Well for one, your leaders are boosting up their military, to counteract military moves by the Japanese leaders and the US leaders.

Let me apologize to all of my messengers. We are not upset at you, and it is our miscalculations that our abduction of you would be enough to keep the piranhas at bay. Obviously, they have short memories, and it is this we want to change."

"What else is going on back there may I ask?" tele-communicated by the Russian astronaut.

"Well, your Leaders are moving into recapture some of the land mass they lost during the Soviet Union collapse, and it is irritating your U.S. counterparts."

"This result is from cosmically unbalanced Starsouls in charge of masses of balanced Starsouls."

"What would happen if you brought us back to Earth now, and we worked with our leaders for peaceful solutions?" Maybe it would take all the attention off the aggression," tele-communicated by Eve, the American astronaut.

"That would not be a good idea at this time. We do not have all of you convinced in our truth, so you cannot convince your leaders. You still have more to learn. We thought this out, and we intend to keep our mission in place."

"It took millions of years to build your world, and we need to finish our mission with you, to stop your leaders from ruining "our fishbowl. How do you know what is happening on our planet all the way out here, millions of light years away?" tele-communicated by the French astronaut.

"We have intergalactic communications with all the worlds, and we have been monitoring developments on these worlds from the beginning of their existence. We understand all languages on your planet Earth. You will find out later that we shaped the direction of your technology."

"Your world is run on Starsouls, and we are the keepers of them. When you totally find out who we are, we will not ask you to go back and spread the word. You will feel it is your human responsibility to do so."

"When we as Soulfurians made this decision to abduct you, we knew this was our last chance to save your world."

"Your world was beyond repair without our help, and we will not rush our process of rejuvenation of humans, because of a few late breaking developments by your Piranha leaders. I brought you all back, because we are concerned that the itchy fingers of your leaders will beat us to the solution."

"With all your power and control of worlds, you must think highly of our human race, to go through the trouble of capturing us, and making us your prophets, so to speak," tele-communicated by the Canadian astronaut.

"Yes exactly, you are learning that the human race is the highlight of our technical accomplishments. You are top on our totem pole, so to speak. You are very lucky to be at this honor and have us watching out for your human race."

"That's why I call you our Spangels, short for space angels," tele-communicated by Eve.

"For now on, after hearing that from our Soulfurian, I would like to take a vote from everyone, on calling them Spangels from this point on."

"Everyone that votes yes, please raise your hands." All at once there was an overwhelming raise of hands in the room. "It is final, now you are our Spangels," tele-communicated Eve.

"This is an honor to be considered by all of you. We work hard to keep you ok, and we will accept your new name for us. When I return to the control room, I will pass this information on to the rest of our Soulfurian crew." "You know they are always watching you as you walk around here, and they are totally amazed at you, as you are at them.

"Well, time has passed on this flight, and now we are coming up to the next planet in this Carnherbivorous Galaxy, to give you a tour of the next part of your Earth's timeline."

"There will be three planets we will visit here. Just look out the window ahead," tele-communicated the Spangel.

"Jurassic to Cretaceous"

"So now we are about two hundred and five million years ago, back on your Planet Earth, with the world brewing with the first mammals, and early smaller dinosaurs. Signs of more global land mass shifted and forming on the interior of the supercontinent Pangea."

"So, we evaluated the life on planet Earth, and calculated in five million years, from that time to around two hundred million years ago, that there would not be enough life to cover all the land separation."

"That is when we traveled back to this upcoming planet for more species of life." As the Soulfurian spacecraft drew closer to the planet Jurrasica, the astronauts could notice the familiar similarities of the atmospheres on every planet they saw, including their planet Earth.

The enormous Starsouls in this atmosphere drew their attention.

It was the same process as the rest of the planets with Starsouls traveling up, down, over and around the atmosphere, like a complete driving force of life around the planet. It was the size of these Starsouls that amazed them.

"We are lowering down to planet Jurrasica," tele-communicated by the Spangel. Here we will hover over the planet for all of you to view the next set of creature Starsouls we implanted into your world, about two hundred and five million years ago."

"Hey, look over there, look at that Stegosaurus," tele-communicated Charles Jones, the English astronaut. 'He has to be eight meters long and weigh two and a half tons."

"Yea look on the ridge over there, it's an Allosaurus. He's about twelve meters long, and weighs about three tons," tele-communicates Alex Roy, the Canadian astronaut.

"Hey there's a Brachiosaurus, that one is humongous. It has to weigh about eighty tons and is about twenty-five meters long."

"I saw this one in that movie Jurassic something, I forgot the name," tele-communicated Adam.

"Let's travel over to the other side of this planet to get a glimpse of some more creatures," tele-communicated the Soulfurian Spangel. The spacecraft lifted in about ten seconds, as they went on to the other side of the planet.

"You see, the continent Pangea back on your planet would be broken into two parts, Gondwana, and Laurasia. We needed to put tall plant eaters on the southern half of the continent, where large jungles would form. "That is why we needed the Brachiosaurus, and all the plant eating creatures of the sauropods," tele-communicated by the Spangel.

"Over here is another herbivore called the Diplodocus. It stands about forty-five meters long, and weighs about thirty tons," tele-communicated the Spangel again.

"Look over there you will see Allosaurus, and Megalosaurus, the bigger dinosaurs. We also took the Starsouls of the first prehistoric birds like Archaeopteryx, and Epidendrosaurus," tele-communicated by the Spangel.

'We transported these Starsouls two hundred and ten million years ago, and it took five million years for these Starsouls to become dinosaurs roaming the planet."

'We needed to populate both continents with dinosaur Starsouls, to keep life evolving on Earth."

"The next planet we extracted Starsouls from we are going to visit now. That planet is the sister planet to this one, and not far away. It is called Cretaceous. We will take a small break, while I help my crew navigate from here to there."

Once again, the Spangel lowered through the floor in his nitrogen filled tube, and left the astronauts gazing at the dinosaur world through the viewing glass.

"This is totally unbelievable," the Russian astronaut tele-communicates." It's like a trip through time, back from the days of Earth's existence."

"Yes, he has very convincingly explained the evolution from reptiles to dinosaurs using his Starsoul theory. Let's see how he ties in life on our planet from the dinosaur age on," tele-communicated by Zhang, the Chinese astronaut. As the astronauts were communicating amongst themselves, the spaceship was pulling away from Planet Jurrasica.

Just then the familiar sound of the Spangel's gas filled tube was on its way up, through the hole in the center of the floor to join them on the third level.

As the tube was rising, the astronauts could see the next planet on the horizon. Once the Spangel was at their level, they were entering the next planet's atmosphere.

It looked just like the last two atmospheres in the Carnherbivorous galaxy.

"Look, there are those Starsouls again, wreaking havoc in this atmosphere," noticed by Haruto, the Japanese astronaut.

"Yes indeed, Starsouls are the common denominator in all galaxies and Solar systems. The Star is the ultimate driving force that supports all life on its planets. Without the star's energy there is no life," tele-communicated by the Soulfurian Spangel.

"Wow, "tele-communicates Charles Jones. "Look at the size of these dinosaurs. They are way bigger than the ones on planet Jurrasica."

"Yes they are, I brought you here just to show all of you the complexity of populating a planet with different species.

I know all the planets in this galaxy are similar, but they are so different," tele-communicated by the Soulfurian Spangel.

"Millions of years before this, we populated your planet until it was completely thriving with reptiles, and a couple of million years later they were completely wiped out by natural planetary evolution, and reformation."

"Luck was on our side millions of years later when we found out there were still reptiles, and birds left alive to transform into Dinosaurs."

"So, millions of years after we introduced Triassic dinosaur Starsouls to your planet's atmosphere, we introduced Jurassica dinosaurs to it."

"The two species Starsouls intermingled and created a lot of new different Dinosaurs.

We topped the planet off around one hundred and forty-four million years ago with the Starsouls from this planet. They turned out to become the most ferocious, and biggest dinosaurs."

"We were very proud of our life accomplishment on planet Earth. Look at some as we tour this planet."

Abelisaurus, Edmontosaurus, Pinacosaurus, Prenocephale Anchiceratops, Erlikosaurus, Prosaurolophus, Ankylosaurus, Euoplocephalus, Protoceratops, Anserimimus, Gallimimus Saichania, Antarctosaurus Garudimimus, Saltasaurus, Aralosaurus, Goyocephale, Saurolophus, Argyrosaurus, Hadrosaurus, Sauroornithoides, Arrhinoceratops, Harpymimus, Segnosaurus, Aublysodon, Homalocephale, Shamosaurus, Avaceratops, Hypacrosaurus, Shanshanosaurus, Avimimus, Kritosaurus, Bactrosaurusrus Triceratops, Denversaurus Pachyrhinosaurus, Trodden, Dromaeosaurus, Panoplosaurus, Velociraptor, Edmontonia, and Pentaceratops.

"These were just some of the Starsouls we implanted into your atmosphere," tele-communicated the Spangel. "As you see here, they are roaming and flying, herbivores, and carnivores."

"One important thing I did not mention was the small creatures you saw on all of these planets in this galaxy, also were collected by us when we were collecting the dinosaur Starsouls. These small creatures were the first mammals that developed alongside the dinosaurs."

"These small creatures were surviving through those millions of years, feeding off the scraps of the plant life that the herbivore dinosaurs left, also the scraps of meat that the Carnivore dinosaurs left, when they were feeding off the herbivores. It was a plentiful ecosystem."

"Most of these prehistoric mammals from this time would eventually lead to your existence, and all of the mammals that are living today on your planet. I will explain all of this in our next briefing. Now I must return to my crew and navigate this spaceship back to Soulfuria. We need to refuel, and re supply food rations before we travel to our next distant galaxies."

"Enjoy these monster dinosaurs, and chat about your thoughts, and what you learned from me. I will see you all back at planet Soulfuria."

The Spangel then lowered his tube through the floor as the astronauts were watching the dinosaurs out of the alien spacecraft window.

"Here we are looking at dinosaurs that roamed our planet up to 65million years ago," tele-communicated by Jeremiah, the American astronaut.

"Yes, and what we are looking at is what our world looked like back then," tele-communicated Jacques the French astronaut.

"This is getting to be more than a history lesson here, it seems he is showing us the meaning of life on our planet, and how it is playing out," tele-communicated by Charles Jones the British astronaut.

"It makes you wonder why though; I can see the whole thing about them being concerned that their "fishbowl," is about to be ruined by the human race."

"Even if that happens, they could start a new species on Earth by what he is saying about Starsoul transfer. Or they can scrap the planet, and watch other planets evolve. My question is why? Why are they so concerned about keeping our planet alive?" tele-communicated by Haruto, the Chinese astronaut.

"Hmmm, that is one very valid question Haruto, and I guess we will have to wait to see what he has in store for us when he returns," tele-communicated Dmitri, the Russian cosmonaut.

"Whatever the reason, I am starting to believe in what I am seeing and hearing," tele-communicated by Maurice, the American astronaut.

As the astronauts were pondering the reason they were abducted, and why they were being placed on this tour, the Soulfurian was busy helping his crews navigate the ship back to planet Soulfuria for refueling.

As we draw our attention to what is happening on planet Earth, there are some late breaking events.

Let's go to the late-night world news report in Toledo Ohio.

"Good evening this is Criss Dromwell, from WGSR in Toledo, bringing you the Late-Night World News Report. As we all know, it's been nine months since the famed alien abduction of twelve astronauts. There have been no accounts of any signs from that and is still a mystery to our planet."

"In other news, tensions are rising in the Middle East, where Israel is threatening to strike the Gaza Strip. Claiming terrorist are strengthening there and are ready to strike Israel."

"In the Koreas, North and South are throwing threats across the Korean Demilitarized Zone. It is a strip of land running across the Korean Peninsula that serves as a buffer zone between North and South Korea."

"The DMZ is a de-facto border barrier, which runs along the 38th parallel."

"Along the Ukrainian front, Russia is still building up troops along its border as the European Union also headed by the United States is tightening sanctions."

"India and Pakistan are breaking down talks between each other, and China is moving military along their southern border."

"The big story tonight is happening in Tehran, Iran, where they are setting up a launch of an intercontinental ballistic missile. They are set to launch this over Turkey, and plan to have it land in the Black sea, as part of a peaceful test they claim."

"Israel and the United states are prepared to shoot the rocket out of the sky once it reaches the black sea. There is protest all over Europe that this test fire can launch a military conflict in the Middle East. We will keep you posted live on any developments."

"Tensions are up on the world stage, and there is no peace in sight. It seems the Spacewalk for Peace was the last time that word peace has made world news."

Now back to the Cosmos to see what the astronauts are doing. The astronauts are all back in their quarters knowing they are on their way to Soulfuria. They know they need to change from their blue jumpsuits to their original space suits. They know they will walk around Soulfuria with their full space suits, and full equipment with oxygen supply tanks, also helmets.

The astronauts were still chatting in telepathy as they were watching space on their way back to Soulfuria.

"How long do you think we have been gone? We have no account of real time. There is no day and night," tele-communicated Eve.

"It's hard to say. It only seems like a few days. We only had slept periods equaling to our time awake. I can't really tell Jersey Girl," tele-communicated by Adam.

"I think we are traveling in space-time, where you are gone away for a short trip, but actually take a long time or something like that," tele-communicated Malone.

"Look out the window, we are coming up on the Soulfurian Galaxy," tele-communicates Jacques the French astronaut.

"Wow, I thought their planet was big the first time we came here, but now we are returning from the other side of the planet. We can see how big their sun is," tele-communicated Maurice.

"It looks like a red giant, and maybe that's why the Soulfurian planet looks so big, by the size of their expanded atmosphere," tele-communicated Axel, the German astronaut.

"The Soulfurian Betrayal"

They were close enough now to see the millions of Starsouls traveling through the Soulfurian atmosphere. There was that buzzer sound again, signaling all the astronauts to report to the lower deck. Once they heard the buzzer, they all went to their transporters, and lowered down.

Once they were all on the lower deck, the head Spangel was there to tell them to suit up with their helmets, and oxygen supply tanks. Then follow the Soulfurian guide to the blue mountain opening, to the left at the space hanger where they were before.

"This is a different route than we took the last time we were here," Adam spoke on his helmet Walkie Talkie.

"Yes, I wonder where, and what they want from us now?" spoken by Malone.

With the crew being on an alien planet, uncertainty was always on the top of their minds. Maurice turned, and looked at the Russian and German astronauts, and they both just shook their head acknowledging, they did not understand where they were.

The astronauts were approaching the blue mountain, there were crowds of Soulfurians in front of the mountain entrance, as if they were making their way in. Also, there were a lot more Soulfurian escorts, as they drew closer to the opening.

The five American astronauts were first in line, they were escorted to the back entrance of the hanger. As they approached the opening, the Soulfurians escorted them through the doors into transport tubes, like in the spacecraft.

These were much bigger, and could fit all twelve, and a few Soulfurian escorts also. They were lifted up to the top level of the mountain. They were led out through a set of double doors, it looked like, but when they reached the doorway the doors just disappeared.

It was like the doors were virtual reality doors. The astronauts made their way inside.

As they were walking, they realized they were on a giant stage. When they looked down, there were thousands of Soulfurians crowding the floor area below. They were not making any verbal noise but were clapping their hands in unison. There was the head Soulfurian on stage with them. The same Spangel they were learning from on the spaceship.

He came from the other direction. There was a virtual screen facing them from the other side of the stage, and the Spangel was standing in the middle of the stage, facing all the Soulfurians in the crowded arena. The Sulfurian escorts lined up the astronauts along the background wall on the stage, so they were standing out in their white spacesuits against the blue background wall.

They could see the Spangel was communicating to the crowd through telepathy, but because the astronauts had to keep their helmets on, they could not sense what he was saying. The virtual screen was displaying what the Spangel was saying in six languages.

It read, "Welcome fellow Soulfurians. I would like to introduce you to our human guest, our "Soulfuturans". The audience erupted in cheers. We acquired them from Planet "Soulfutura."

The Soulfurian crowd was clapping like crazy. They were very glad the astronauts were there. The astronauts were shocked, it seemed all their questions were just answered by the one line from the Spangel to the Soulfurians.

April was the first to speak, "I'm taking back the Spangel name from him now. There's no way a Spangel would double cross us like this, "Soulfuturans" and "Soulfutura."

I guess we all know what that means." Maurice spoke next, "I had a feeling about this alien, that he was not being upfront with us."

The head Soulfurian told the crowd that the astronauts were in training to send back the ultimatum to their Planet Soulfutura.

Malone said, "He never mentioned any ultimatum to us in his teachings."

Adam said, "How dare him humiliate us like this, to his fellow Soulfurians."

All the other astronauts looked confused from what the lead Soulfurian is doing. It seemed like what the leader was saying to make the astronauts uncomfortable, was making his fellow Soulfurians very happy.

He was explaining to the crowd how they captured the astronauts, and how he was showing them how the Soulfurian aliens were in total control of life on their planet, also how through Starsoul technology, he was educating them.

Also, how he was preparing them to take their ultimatum back to their planet to tell the leaders they are called Soulfuturians.

The Soulfurian aliens were clapping with approval of what the leader Sulfurian was telling them. Then all at once the escort Soulfurians gestured to the astronauts to walk straight off the stage to a room to the side.

Eve was furious, she felt like she was being put on display with no warning by the leader Soulfurian. Maurice had a cooler head telling Eve to keep cool. The worst thing she could do now, was to embarrass the leader in front of his alien friends and wait until they arrived back on the spaceship.

Once the astronauts were off the stage, and standing in the staging room, the escorts showed them the way to the transporter. The astronauts followed the escorts to the transporter.

They transported down and went back out the backdoors of the big blue mountain opening.

They were headed back to the supply hanger, over by the alien spaceship.

They were going between the buildings, when Malone noticed the Soulfurian ship was just resting on a giant granite stone triangle.

They didn't see this angle coming from the other direction, the first time they were here. "Do you see that?" He points to the spacecraft docking on the giant stone structure.

"That stone structure the spaceship is docked on looks awful familiar. I can't put my finger on it, but we can get a better look at it when we take off."

The Soulfurian escorts led the astronauts to the mountain hanger building. The only building they were allowed at, the last time they were here.

They all entered the building where Soulfurians were entering and exiting with these glass canisters.

The canisters they use to capture, and transport Starsouls.

Eve said to Malone through her space helmet mike, "I wonder how they capture those Starsouls, they travel so fast it seems impossible."

Malone replies, "They must have had a lot of practice after a million years or so."

The escorts led the astronauts to the electronic commissary room, where they all ordered their food rations. Adam was filling his bag, and said, "Where is the leader at?" He was here last time to guide us."

"This time we have the escorts to show us the way." Eve replied, "He probably headed back to the spaceship. He must know he pissed us off."

Maurice stepped to Eve and whispered, "Let's not show these Soulfurians our disappointment with their leader at this time. We may never make it back to the ship."

Once all the astronauts had their rations, the Soulfurian escorts led them out the main entrance.

Once again, like the last time they were here, the Soulfurians were gathering around the astronauts like they were zoo animals. As they were hopping back to the spacecraft, the Soulfurians clapped like they were happy to see them go.

Jeremiah yelled in his helmet microphone, "It was nice to see you too. I hope we never come back here again."

"Now, now," said Maurice. They were very polite to us, just wave to them and smile." The astronauts filed one by one back into the spacecraft.

They took off their space gear after they received the ok. The lower level was filled with the right oxygen levels. They each grabbed their bags, and headed back to their transporters, then up to their quarters.

The Soulfurian space crew was just finishing loading the new fuel rods to the spaceship, to power them on to their next flight and destination.

Eve was settled in her quarters; she was just finishing changing into her blue jumpsuit when she felt a sudden jolt under her feet. It was the spaceship lifting off.

Just at that moment the bell went off to signal the astronauts back up to the top level. Malone was the first to make it to his transporter and take it to the third level. Once he reached the third level he saw the Soulfurian leader there waiting for them already.

He then ran to the spaceship window and looked down. "I knew it, I frigging knew it," he tele-communicated.

He then stared out the window until the others arrived. "What are you staring at?" Zhang tele-communicated to Malone." Pyramids," Malone answered.

"What do you mean?" tele-communicated Axel, the German astronaut.

"Look down at the takeoff area, all these spaceships use pyramids as their landing pods," tele-communicated Malone.

Everyone else was there by then, and they all looked out the window to get a look.

"Boy this is like a movie, you ever watch a movie, and then the second time you watch it you notice things for the first time? This is what it feels like," tele-communicated Adam.

"Look, they are all different sizes too," tele-communicated Haruto, the Japanese astronaut.

"Primatourious"

"2,300,000 building blocks, weighing an average of 2.5 tons each, was the formula for one of your seven wonders of your world. The first and biggest pyramid built in Giza, about four thousand five hundred and sixty-five years ago. I believe this was the time when we helped your kind to construct one of our landing pods," tele-communicated the Soulfurian.

That statement combined with them seeing the pyramids on Soulfuria, immediately erased any doubts, or suspicions the astronauts had in the Soulfurian leader steering them the wrong way. They suddenly realized by that statement, the Soulfurian had a lot more to educate them on. Any anger at the Soulfurian for what he did to the astronauts on planet Soulfuria was immediately extinguished.

"Ok, now I have everyone's attention, let me start where I left off at our last meeting. Dinosaurs and mammals of all kinds roamed your planet for another one hundred fifty-five million years."

Just about that period of time our Soulfurian geologist were reporting to us that our Star was expanding. It meant ultimately that our planet Soulfuria, and all of us Soulfurians would eventually cease to exist."

"It will take millions of years until our Star burns off our nitrogen atmosphere, but ultimately this will be the end for our species."

"Now being one of the Big Bang's first galaxies formed, we understood that eventually the original galaxies' Stars formed, would eventually die. We as Soulfurians, keepers of the galaxies' Starsouls, had too much responsibility to just eventually fade away."

"We needed to come up with a long-time future plan for the continuance of the Soulfurian species."

"We needed to find another planet that had the same makeup of an atmosphere as our planet, somewhere in the latter part of the Big Bang where the Stars are young. We searched for thousands of years and could not find one."

"Until one day, one of our scientific Soulfurians, came up with a Trans World Blueprint for our future existence, on a planet that was close to our atmospheric composition. The whole time searching for this planet, we had your planet under our nose the whole time."

"That's when we named your planet Soulfutura."

"Cold goose bump chills just ran down every spine of the astronauts. Soulfuturians was the name the Leader Soulfurian referred to the astronauts as, in front of a crowd back on Soulfuria.

"You mean planet Earth?" tele-communicated Maurice.

"Exactly," tele-communicated the Soulfurian.

"Ok, then that answers the why you care so much for our planet surviving. You are not just keepers of Starsouls, this is personal for the Soulfurians," tele-communicated Maurice.

"Also correct my student. Now I need everyone to focus out the window to the planet we are about to come up on."

The astronauts looked out the window as the spaceship was closing in on a planet that looked just like their planet Earth.

"For a minute here, I could swear this is our planet Earth," tele-communicated Jacques, the French astronaut.

"Very close to Earth is this planet, because it is the same distance away from its Star as Earth is to your Sun. It has the exact same atmosphere as Earth, and you humans can live, and breathe on this planet, but it is too populated with an abundance number of primates.

This planet is called "Primatourious."

"The astronauts could see all the Starsouls controlling the atmosphere, and traveling throughout the skies, as the spaceship was descending. When the spaceship reached a certain level they could scan the planet. The only life on this planet was primates. These primates were never seen by man before. They were a weird species that looked like cats and dogs with four legs and tails but resembled the makeup of monkeys.

"You say these are primates, but they are not familiar to the primates on our planet," tele-communicated Malone.

"But they are," tele-communicated the Sulfurian. "They are primates, they are the original primates that evolved into many species of primates, including Gorilla, Orangutan, Chimpanzee, and Hominids."

"The latter Hominids eventually evolved to Homo erectus, Neanderthal and Homo sapiens."

"Well, if your Soulfurian world was looking for a planet to transfer to, why didn't you pick this planet?" tele-communicated Charles, the British astronaut.

"This planet did not meet our plans criteria. It has an older Star formed at the beginning of the big bang like ours, so it would not work," tele-communicated the Soulfurian.

"The one thing about this planet that did fit in our transformation plan was, we found a species that we could work with as our future."

"These Starsouls have been very valuable to our Soulfurian species that the inventor of this master regeneration plan became our new planet leader."

His name is"Ra."

"Ra, the Egyptian sun God?" tele-communicated Maurice.

"Yes, he is the sun god that was worshipped for centuries by your Egyptians. We will get to that later in my teachings."

"Our master transformation was underway, and we had the species we were looking to transform, and we had our planet to transfer too."

"The problem came when we had to transfer these primate Starsouls to Planet Soulfutura's atmosphere."

"The planet was overrun by carnivorous dinosaurs with hundreds of millions of years to thrive. There was no way we could add these Starsouls. "The only solution to extend the species of Soulfurians was to eliminate the species, and Starsouls of the dinosaurs without eliminating the mammal species on the planet."

"Around sixty-six million years ago, we took a whole fleet of Soulfurian spacecraft, and lined them in various positions along the asteroid belt in your solar system. Once in place we started Project Renew."

"This project would eliminate the dinosaur species from your planet, and most mammals would also suffer the same fate, all in the name of Soulfurian survival"

"It was a three-step approach to eliminate a species of animals that evolved for millions of years. In step one, what we did was aimed our powerful lasers at the large asteroids in your solar systems asteroid belt and blew them apart into meteorites and directed them at your planet. We needed to strike all parts of the planet in order to basically choke the atmosphere of dinosaur Starsouls, along with blocking the sunlight from the planet."

"Step two, was Earth's reaction to the asteroid impacts. It's volcano's started erupting everywhere causing more toxic gases to the atmosphere."

"Between the two, the sunlight was blocked for years, causing global cooling effects that wiped a lot of dinosaur species out."

"Of course, all the toxic gases in the air wiped out all dinosaur Starsouls."

"Step three, was the period we put on the global destruction, and that was a six-mile asteroid that we deflected down to your New Mexico area that put an exclamation mark on our mission. That is what we meant by renew."

"The plan proceeded, and the process was complete about sixty-five million years ago. This would be called by your human race as the KT extinction event. We waited one half million years for the atmosphere to clear. When all the dust cleared, some animal and plant life that survived the extinction was revived once again."

"One benefit from the KT extinction we did not calculate, was the new Starsouls added to your atmosphere."

"It was the asteroids and meteorites that destroyed the dinosaurs, also filled the atmosphere with advanced mammal Starsouls that was locked in them, leftover from your solar system development, and locked in various cosmic rocks."

"That changed the makeup of a lot of mammal Starsouls, and changed them to new animal Starsouls."

"What that meant was by the time of sixty-four million years ago, these new mammal Starsouls would attach themselves to newly formed animal offspring and start a mammal explosion on your planet."

"Also, new species of animals would develop from this renewal of life on your planet. The time was right for us to start introducing primate Starsouls, to mix in your atmosphere with existing mammal type Starsouls, so that primates could start evolving on your planet."

"Are there any questions my students?"

"That would explain the explosion of many species of animals during the Cambrian explosion, that there were no previous fossils found," tele-communicated Maurice.

"Yes, a very strange occurrence went on during a million years of different cosmically balanced Starsouls of different size, and makeup."

"Mixing and clashing following the asteroid meteorite bombardment of your planet."

"There was a planet-wide iridium layer snowing down from the fallout, erasing fossils of mammal development in that period," the Soulfurian tele-communicated. "Are there any more questions?"

"Yes, so let me get this straight, You Soulfurians, introduced reptiles, then dinosaurs, and mammals. Then you wiped out the dinosaurs, and most mammals, and now the KT extinction was your renewal of life project to introduce new animals, and primates to the planet all with Starsouls?" tele-communicated Adam.

"Well yes, in the beginning your planet was just a thriving planet with one of the youngest Stars sustaining life. We were proud to keep life alive and thriving on your world until the day we received news that our world was in jeopardy."

"We found our star was one of the oldest in the galaxies from the original big bang."

"That is when our now leader Ra, came up with the, "Trans Soulfurian World Blueprint" to renew our continued existence."

"We needed three ingredients for this transition to happen. We needed a non-hostile world, which the KT extinction brought. Then we needed to find a creature that resembles our cosmic and physical makeup. That was the placement of primate Starsouls into your atmosphere."

"When I return, I will teach you the final phase of our eternal transformation. So now I need to attend to my crew and set our course to your neighbor galaxy Andromeda."

The leader Soulfurian lowers into the floor as the astronauts mull over his teachings. "Andromeda, does that mean we are headed home?" tele-communicated Axel, the German astronaut. "Yes, it seems that way. I think in the next session he is about to drop the bomb on explaining our existence," tele-communicated Adam.

"The Cosmic Instruction"

"If he does that, I will have a big problem with him playing God, and claiming not to be God," tele-communicated Jeremiah.

"Well, that subject was broached before, and he made a very good point by using our technology of stem cell research, to question us if we would call ourselves God, and for being able to create life scientifically with test tube babies," tele-communicated Maurice.

"I am so confused right now, I don't know what to believe. I was taught one way to believe, and now I am being showed another. The hard part is, this way makes more sense to me," tele-communicated Eve.

"Yes, with the Starsoul evidence, it is hard to say no," tele-communicated Malone. "Let's just hear his story out before we make any decisions. I still must hear the missing link. Now I am getting sleepy and heading for my room."

That was the key for everyone to wind down and get rest. While the astronauts are resting, and the Soulfurians are guiding their spaceship, we will break away to planet Earth, to see any new developments.

Welcome to WSBC evening news with Sara Char, and Steve Glenna, here in Santa Barbara California.

"The top stories tonight will be the terrible weather we have been experiencing here, also the latest development around the world with the Superpower's crisis."

"Also talking about our around the world space segment, where we will unveil that N.A.S.A. has a new signal tower built, that can not only travel around the world, but around the universe."

"I can't wait until we get to that segment", explained reporter Char. "Let's start out with reporter Steve Glenna out there in the rain battling fierce winds."

"Thank you, Sara, good evening folks, as you know this rain has been hitting us hard for the past three days with flood levels reaching critical stages. I am by a main highway, where you can see the rain and water running right over it. There have been numerous power outages as we endure this storm. Stay tuned at the end of this broadcast, for a more detailed update when this storm will leave us. Now back to you Sara."

"In world news, all the Superpowers are holding a summit on all the differences they have between them, in two months from now. They are trying to diffuse a worldwide crisis on military occupation, and nuclear submarine maneuvers around the globe."

"The Chinese are at difference with Japan for bolstering their military forces, a move looked at by the Chinese to be a threat to the motherland."

"Also, Russia's disagreement with the United States, has forced sanctions on both sides over the land dispute in Ukraine."

"India and Pakistan are at arms over Kashmir, with both countries showing their military muscle."

"Israel and Syria are throwing words of war across the land, it seems this summit coming is the last chance for world peace, or it will be the last meeting before a worldwide military conflict. It seems everything is coming to a head at this upcoming summit."

"Finally, before sports and weather we save the best story for last. Remember ten months ago, our five American and seven European astronauts were suddenly snatched up from outer space by rogue aliens."

"It was an event that changed us forever. Well, N.A.S.A. headquarters in Florida and Houston Texas, have been working on a special communication device for the international space station."

"Let's go to Houston Texas to get an update from the chief spokesman of N.A.S.A."

"Good evening all, you great citizens around the world. My name is Joseph C. Driver Jr. Thank you in advance for the opportunity to speak on behalf of N.A.S.A, and the International Space Community."

"Since we have experienced the disappearance of our twelve young astronauts, and the same astronauts we have been calling our twelve angels, who left this world in the name of world peace to better mankind, we have been building a communication satellite, specially designed to send a never ending signal out to the universe."

"A signal that reads in Morse code: "BRING OUR ANGELS HOME." This satellite has the power to reach the far depths of the great universe, and circle three hundred sixty degrees, to put our signal everywhere in space. Hoping wherever the extraterrestrials took them, they could hear our plea to get our angels back home."

"It's a real shot in the dark, but that's all we have right now. In one week, we will reveal the satellite, and power it up for the first time."

"It will be a message heard around the cosmos. We are here with the International Space Community and are dedicated to getting our astronauts back. We will not quit and will search the stars for how long it takes. You heard it first right here, from WSBC evening news, with Sara Char and Steve Glenna, here in the Santa Barbara California. We will go to sports right after a few messages from our sponsors."

Meanwhile, back on the Soulfurian spacecraft the astronauts heard the alarm buzzer once more, as it meant the head Soulfurian was waiting for them on the third level once again. Once the astronaut crew returned to the space view floor, the Soulfurian eyed them up from left to right, and gave them a thumb up. That broke the tension they had with the Sulfurian after hearing his actual plan for their planet.

The Sulfurian then started with, "While you were all resting, we returned back through the black hole we first went through on our journey to Soulfuria."

"Does that mean you are taking us back to Earth?" tele-communicated Charles.

"Not so fast, I don't have everyone's total faith yet. I still have more to teach you, so you can teach your human race," tele-communicated the Soulfurian. "Ok, the trip to Andromeda is a long ride. It is the last solar system we will visit before I send you back to lead with our instruction."

"You mean an ultimatum for our people," tele-communicated Axle.

"Yes, I know I used those words communicating to my people, but put yourself in my place, I am sent out to save a world from self-destruction, and it happens to be the same world that my Soulfurian race hopes to inhabit in the future," tele-communicate the Soulfurian leader.

"Let's get back to where I left off at our last session. Around sixty-four million years ago your planet was thriving without dinosaurs, and developing new life through new mammals, and animals that would eventually lead to the ones walking today. Well, the same is so for the first primates that roamed your planet. I will show you how we evolved these primates to human form in a matter of six million years."

"Ok, there you go again with how you Soulfurians put us on our planet. That statement draws the line, of what we believe is the work of our God," tele-communicated Jeremiah.

"There you go, with the word God again. That is what your Egyptians called our leader Ra. That was also how other civilizations referred to us through various ages of the human lifeline."

"Well, I speak for my people and declare we are not Gods. Why is it you humans can design or assign God just to care for life on just your planet? God is great!"

"He created the Big Bang, he created all the galaxies, and he created all the stars, all the solar systems, and all planets. He even created our planet right after the big bang. He created us about ten billion years ago".

"What is so hard to believe that God is a lot bigger and more capable than you think? To believe you are the only life in the cosmos would not be doing God justice."

"What is so hard to believe that we could evolve ten billion years ago, in one of the earliest galaxies, and solar systems created by the big bang?"

"Why is it so hard to believe that after that amount of time, our technology is where it is today?"

"After watching your technology develop in just six million years, why would you believe that after ten billion years when our Star dies, that we are not capable of relocating our race on a planet suitable for our living, and on a planet with one of the youngest stars in the solar system?"

"Why it is so hard to believe that part of our plan is to see the human race survive, and thrive, and live in perfect harmony just like we live. We are more worried about your planet's self-destruction, more than your human race is. Your humankinds are future Soulfurians."

"I will teach you how we evolved humans, and I will teach you what humans will eventually look like and show you how the human race is going to evolve to become us."

"I want you to think about what your ancestors looked like, when they evolved from hominids. Then look how your appearance changed from that."

"Losing most body hair and look how fast your technology advanced in the last six million years. Picture what your future generations will evolve to."

"Picture eventually your human race losing all body hair like us. Picture your Earth's atmosphere losing its ozone layer, causing you to wear these black protective lenses, blocking UV rays, and preventing your retinas from burning out like ours."

Just then the Soulfurian popped his black eyeball caps off, and he had eye's just like the astronauts. They were in shock.

"Picture your brain getting bigger, causing your skull to enlarge like us, and when your human race develops the ability to communicate in telepathy like us."

"Picture your mouths and ears evolving to grow smaller because there is no longer a need to talk and listen. Picture your fingers growing fatter on the tips, because of your future generations will communicate globally with pads and texting."

"Picture your genitalia becoming obsolete, and eventually evolving away, because of the ability to reach orgasm through mental telepathy. Just looking, and mentally communicating with your partner would be all you need to do."

"Now picture the future Human, would it be fair to call them future Soulfurians then. Would it be fair to say the human race is about halfway to looking like us now?"

"Oh, these protective eye caps also give us the ability to see Starsouls."

"Our hope is that your human race will believe in the Starsoul, and that living an equally balanced life of basic good intentions will keep their Starsouls free for eternity."

"Yes, when we send you back to your planet, we will give each of you the Starsoul facts to live by. This will be called "The Starsoul Instruction."

"It's to teach your people to live in peace, and not just do a spacewalk for peace, as you started out.

You will be key in our plan, to make your world live in peace. I will give you the power to make this happen, so don't consider it an ultimatum. We are coming up on the Galaxy Andromeda soon now."

"Why are we going to the Andromeda galaxy before going home?" tele-communicated Haruto.

"Do you see how you have your Hollywood? Well, we have planets in the Andromeda galaxy that we like to set up scenes on, like you do in Hollywood."

" We developed a virtual world you can walk about, and experience for yourself."

"We can create these shows of worlds, using laser technology like you never seen before. It is our way of showing you a good experience, after all you been through. Also, a break from what you are about to embark on. We want to explain our involvement on your human development, as we did in the last six million years of human existence."

"We believe after we leave the Andromeda galaxy, your minds will be made up to join our cause, and better your human race."

"We picked a planet in the solar system because its galaxy is also like your planet with deserts, and oceans, and landscapes like your Earth. Also, the atmosphere is good for you too."

"Then why don't you take over that planet instead of ours. It also has a young star too?" tele-communicated by Dmitri.

"We did look at that possibility, but after future review, we calculated that the galaxy Andromeda will eventually collide with the Milky Way galaxy, and this planet will not survive the collision, but your planet Earth will in all our calculations."

"Boy that is good news, I'm sure that will make our scientist happy back home," tele-communicated Adam.

"Well, here we are, Galaxy Andromeda. Now we will head on down to planet X41 on our cosmic map,' tele-communicated the Soulfurian leader.

The astronauts all looked out the window, and there were those Starsouls again just flooding the atmosphere of this alien planet. They were all excited to be one step closer to home.

Just then the spaceship landed, and the Soulfurian leader led the astronauts to exit the spaceship.

"Soulfuture Evolution"

They were told they can exit the craft in their jumpsuits, with no breathing apparatus necessary. So all the astronauts made their way down to level one, and one by one made it out onto the planet surface.

They all gathered outside the spacecraft, a Soulfurian escort led them away from the spacecraft. It was the first time they were outside with no real space suits on, and the Soulfurian was wearing breathing apparatus." Wow, this feels a lot like Earth," said Eve. "Yea we could actually talk to each other out here," said Jeremiah. "This is unbelievable," said Maurice.

The astronauts were discovering how they could talk to one person, and still communicate through telepathy to another at the same time.

The Americans were talking to each other, and they were realizing the foreign astronauts understood what they were saying.

The Soulfurian led the astronauts over a ridge on the alien landscape, and once they crossed over, they could see there was a natural coliseum like theater down below.

The Soulfurian pointed to the seating area for the astronauts to go to. The place looked like a Roman Coliseum with an alien twist. All the astronauts took a seat. They all were comfortable in their seating. Out of nowhere from the center stage, on the theater floor below them, in this vast theater, the lead Soulfurian rose up from below the staging area in his glass tube. Like the same tube he had on the Soulfurian spaceship.

"Welcome my Soulfuturains" was the telepathy message he sent to them, as he looked up and panned his eyes from left to right. "How do you all like our virtual reality coliseum?"

They were all in shock once again.

"What do you mean this coliseum is real?" telecommunicated Maurice.

"Real, don't be silly, this is what virtual reality will be like for your future generations. It will be so advanced after your future generations learn fourth and fifth dimensional staging," tele-communicated the Soulfurian leader.

"We are sitting on seats, if this is virtual reality, how can it support our weight?" tele-communicated Malone.

"Yes, it's all built around lasers with bending light that can support matter. It's too much to explain. Let's get the show started down here in the staging area."

"We made a presentation for you, to show you the timeline of our influence, in the steps we took to bring Earth into your twenty-first century, way back from about sixty-five million years ago."

"There are pairs of glasses I need all of you to wear during this presentation."

"They are in the armrest to your left. This will enable you to view Starsouls, like you did in the spacecraft."

"There will be virtual presentations down on the ground level below, and when the lighting dims, there will be virtual monitors communicating what is happening, in each of your individual languages."

"After the show is over, I will be back to go over this segment, and answer questions. Sit back, learn, and enjoy." The Soulfurian then lowered his tube.

Adam, in his "John Wayne" voice said, "Where is the popcorn and soda pop cowboy?"

Seems his humor was coming back, the closer he was getting to Earth. All the astronauts relaxed back as the lighting dimmed, and the virtual screens turned on in front.

They were like Teleprompters with voice over air capabilities.

"Welcome Humans and fellow Soulfuturans" That was the first sounds coming from the monitor,

"It was about sixty-four million years ago, after the KT extinction, the Soulfurian starships deposited primate Starsouls into Earth's atmosphere." The astronauts were in awe, because as the monitor was talking, they were watching the starships do the depositing of Starsouls overhead.

All mammals were on the ground, and there were some they never seen before.

The monitor reported, "It took about a thousand years for the transformation of primate Starsouls to resonate in early mammals, and evolve into living breathing primates of all kinds, and to roam planet Earth."

Then they showed real live primates swinging and climbing trees on the ground.

The monitor continued, "The Soulfurians waited for thirty-four million years for the primates to multiply in numbers, until they started the third process of their "Tran World Soulfurian Blueprint," of the eternal transformation of Soulfurians."

Then on the ground, the astronauts could see there was a virtual timeline of monkeys, with tails called new world monkeys, called Aegyptopithecus. The monitor continued, "They were not far evolved from the mammals called Carpolestes simpsoni. They were their thirty million year predecessor. They eventually split into two groups, Old world monkeys (Cercopithecoidea) and Apes (Hominoidea)."

The Soulfurian starships were highlighting these primates with lasers. The monitor continued, "This time was about twenty-five million years ago." While the lasers were still focused on the Catarrhini below.

The Soulfurians watched these Aegyptopithecus evolve for millions of years. After ten million years of slow growth, and advancement the creatures advanced to upright walking Hominoidea, as they became the Sahelanthropus tchadensis."

They showed a specimen on the ground. The monitor continued, "For the next ten million years, these creatures then evolved to   Australopithecus afarensis, a creature that walked upright and had smaller teeth."

They highlighted with lasers of what that creature looked like.

The monitor continued, "This is when the Soulfurians had enough of this slow growing, slow evolving species, and started the next phase of their regeneration. This was a time around two point five, to one point eight million years ago, Soulfurian starships gathered over Earth's atmosphere."

All the astronauts looked up to about a million alien spaceships covering the skies above. With the addition of the sunglasses they were given, they started to see exactly what the Soulfurian space crafts were there to do. They released Soulfurian Starsouls into the atmosphere.

The voice from the monitor started again, "About five hundred thousand years later, the Soulfurian Starsouls were finding fertile Australopithecus afarensis females, and residing in the newborn creatures. Quickly, the creatures evolved to Homo habilis and Homo erectus, also Homo pekinensis that first appeared in Asia."

The lasers then highlighted these creatures. The monitor voice continued, "About another million years of more Soulfurian Starsouls being planted in Earth's atmosphere had the Homo erectus developing into Homo heidelbergensis."

When they brought this creature out you could see the human resemblance.

He looked like a cave man with a lot less body hair, and upright walking holding primitive tools.

The monitor voice continued, "He looked Neanderthal, and his kind has migrated all over the globe. They grew to gain the technology of tools and using fire for thousands of years."

"They made shelters and lived in groups and family settings."

"Then finally about one hundred thousand years ago with thousands of years of offspring being born with Soulfurian Starsouls, the once Australopithecus afarensis became the first Neanderthal, who evolved to the first Homo sapiens."

They then brought out the first Homo sapiens on the ground, it looked like a naked man and woman standing there on the ground. The monitor announced, "Here are the first Adam and Eve."

The astronauts were once again in complete awe. They watched the process of Soulfurian Starsouls coming down from the sky and the pregnant Hominids breathe them in.

And a newer more advanced species be born over and over again through the generations. Now they saw with their own eyes the transformation from Australopithecus afarensis to man with the power of Soulfurian Starsouls.

Just then the stage below dimmed, and the seating lights came on. Then the Soulfurian glass cylinder rose once again. The lead Soulfurian panned at the astronauts and saw the astronauts were in complete shock.

The Soulfurian leader tele-communicated, "Is there anyone with any questions on the presentation."

Adam was first to ask, "This presentation just seemed so real life like. Homo erectus you imply, spawned from of the Australopithecus afarensis. Was that the first line of species that received Soulfurian Starsouls?

The Soulfurian leader tele- communicated, "Yes this was the time to start introducing Soulfurian Starsouls into the atmosphere, to infuse into a primate that was not an ape, not a monkey, and not an orangutan. This creature was a species evolved from the great apes, not spawned from an ape."

"Homo erectus, Homo Neanderthal and Homo sapiens are cousins of the Apes and Chimpanzees. That is why Apes and Orangutans, and Chimpanzees still are a different species walking your planet today."

"We put primate Starsouls in Earth's atmosphere eighty-five million years ago. Hominids changed little in appearance or advancement as a species, until we introduced Soulfurian Starsouls to Earth's atmosphere, about six million years ago. Now I say look at yourselves as humans today."

"Look how far your advancement in appearance and technology has developed in those six million years.

Look how far you have advanced in your last one hundred years, and you tell me it hasn't come from a more intelligent species."

"So, your kind created man and God didn't?" tele-communicate Jeremiah.

The Soulfurian leader tele-communicated, "There you go again thinking God is just meant for creating life on Earth, and not for the whole universe. God had created us way before we created you, so technically God did create you, because he created everything before you.

Knowing no other life, it would be natural to for your humans to believe that God is just your creator."

"Now I hope after we finish with your humankind and send them on their way to peace and prosperity, they will have their eyes open to how great their God is."

"Ok, your name is back to Spangel." Maybe God saw what would happen with our world, on its way to nuclear destruction, and then made the Soulfurian Star die out, so it would force the Soulfurians to come here, and make our world right. That would be you doing God's work, but not communicating with God, so that would make you our space angels," tele-communicated Eve.

"I believe the peace the Soulfurians have showed us on this trip, is the same peace we all went to space for," tele-communicated Haruto.

"Well, it's about time, I have two of you convinced in our mission." ," tele-communicated the leader Soulfurian. "I think you have more than two of us on board," tele-communicated Maurice.

"We just took a vote, and after what we have been through, and after everything we have seen with our own eyes, you showed us the drastic change from Hominid to Human."

"In just a few thousand years, and after no change in hominids for millions, we are totally unanimously devoted to joining you in this mission, to convince our leaders to disarm."

"Are there any other things Soulfurians have been involved in human times since the first Homo sapiens?" tele-communicated Adam.

"Yes, as a matter of fact we have been periodically visiting your humankind throughout the ages. We have had communications with every civilization, and each individual human looking to the sky and nighttime stars for knowledge."

"As we found all of you in space hoping for world peace. There were times, sometimes your Egyptian civilization would call our Starships, "Chariots of fire."

"Well, we have been periodically, over the past four thousand years, releasing Soulfurian Starsouls in your atmosphere. That means that everything man has been doing in the past four thousand years is our involvement in human times."

"We have been watching your skies for centuries. We have picked up transmissions from Earth, about sightings of us throughout. "We used telepathy to communicate with thousands of humans for the betterment of technology and knowledge. We gave the Egyptians, The Mayans, and the Incas, the knowledge of the building of the pyramids. "

"We constantly monitor the skies of your world for any human seeking knowledge, as we did in the past, up until this modern day."

"People you consider genius have good things going for them. At birth, they acquired one of the oldest Soulfurian Starsouls."

"It resided in their pineal glands in the center of their brains, with an outstanding effect on the human that received it, with exceptional knowledge. A perfect example would be, Albert Einstein."

"Thousands of older Soulfurian Starsouls took on human life enabling the Soulfurian knowledge to be shared with the human species."

"Between all of these Soulfurian Starsouls, and visits from us communicating through telepathy, your human technology has jumped ahead in leaps and bounds in the last four thousand years in the lifetime of humanity.

"Pictures have been drawn of us, since the beginning of time in caves till these present days, in books and movies."

"It's funny how all the drawings of us look the same throughout time and cultures. Humans are the ancestors of future Soulfurians."

"Now you know who we are, and why we are here, and why we abducted you, I think you know who you are and why you are here and are now ready for the next step."

"We will be taking you back home soon. We are getting signals on our communication receivers displaying your humanity's world's plea to bring their angels home. "Look for yourself," tele-communicated the Spangel.

Just then the Soulfurian showed the astronauts the satellite at the International Space Station on the monitor. They were all glad to see something from home again. They were assured that the world was still looking for them.

"Since I have all of you convinced of the Starsouls, and the purpose of humanity and Soulfuria, there will be no more need for proof."

"This tour, and journey is officially over, and you will go back home. All twelve of you are the first Soulfuturans of all of humanity."

"It will be your job to lead your people. Your people sent you to space for an answer to peace, through your spacewalk for peace."

"We have heard your plea, and educated you on the true meaning of peace, through Starsouls. We are sending you all back as leaders, to teach your world the only way to live forever, is to keep your Starsoul cosmically balanced."

"When you convince your entire world that is when your world will live in peace. We as Soulfurians will go back to our planet, and let evolution take its course."

"In order to make this mission successful, we need to take some measures so you will be able to lead. I, the leader of the Soulfurian Star fleet has the honor of anointing all twelve of you "Earth's New World Order." You will be stronger than any leader on Earth."

"The masses will follow you in our teachings. There is no military on Earth that can stop you."

"When we return you to Earth, we are expecting a great welcome back in order for you. It is this time you need to seize the opportunity to take control. You are the new peacemakers for your planet. We expect opposition after the celebrating is done. We don't expect your leaders to comply with your instructions. This is where we will wait to assist you."

"When the world leaders see the support you will have, they will have no choice to join the masses in following you. This is a mission of peace. We will show your world that peace can prevail without any killing. We have the technology to make this happen. We need you to return, and lead your nations to disarm all nuclear weapons, which are the ultimate weapons of mass destruction."

"Nuclear energy technology was meant for a fuel source, not weapons. We will teach your humankind how to control without killing. "

"There will be times when you will need our help on your task. We will be with you every step of the way. We will not leave your side until your world is at peace."

"Once you show your world the way, they will listen. Get ready to be famous, but I will caution you, fame has its responsibilities. The world's eyes will be on you for the rest of your lives."

"I'm sure you will have many questions for me, and I will be glad to answer them while I prepare you for your return. Right now, we need to get back to the spacecraft, and be on our way. I will now ask you to return and get ready for your mission, as we get the spacecraft ready to return you to your planet."

The astronauts all obliged and made their way back to the spacecraft. They were excited they were going back home, and very aware of their mission.

It seems the astronauts have one hundred percent confidence in their new friends from the cosmos.

On the way back to the spaceship, Jeremiah says to Eve, "Well it looks like they did it." They showed us our origins and explained to us why we are getting more and more intelligent at an alarming rate, compared to our ancestors."

Eve replied to Jeremiah, "Yes compare our advancement in the past hundred years to the advancement of our ancestors over millions of years."

The Soulfurian spacecraft started its silent engines and lifted off from planet X41. It was headed to the Milky Way Galaxy. The astronauts were waiting eagerly on the spacecraft's third observation level, for the lead Soulfurian to emerge.

"What do you think he wants us to do?" tele-communicated Eve.

"He wants us to lead the world with this Starsoul belief," tele-communicated Maurice.

"He is right, we went to space for peace, and he will give us the power to keep the peace on Earth. I'm looking forward to this," tele-communicated Axel.

"Hey, we started our mission for international peace, and that is exactly what the Soulfurians want. I think if there is a way we could achieve this, the Soulfurians will be on their way, and our world will be peaceful," tele-communicated Dmitri. "Let's just wait and see what his plan is before we jump the gun here," tele-communicated Adam. "Yea, I wonder how he is going to make us so powerful, that all the world militaries will listen," tele-communicated Haruto.

Just as the astronauts were speaking, the Soulfurian glass tube arose from the floor, and met them on the third level.

"The Cosmic Homecoming"

"Ok, my humans, Soulfuturans, Let's get this meeting started." It was the first thoughts communicated by the Soulfurian Leader. "Here are our plans for you."

"What I have in my hands is the Soulfurian laws of Starsouls called, "The Starsoul Instruction." This is on a circuit chip I have for you to display to your Human race. You just press this button on this chip, and a virtual display screen will appear. That should get your human audience's attention."

"Once you play this video to your human media, you will have millions of instant supporters. Also, you will have millions in disbelief. This will be a trying time between the believers and the non-believers. This is when I will need all of you to calm the masses, and take control of the masses, at the same time."

"All you have to do is confirm what is in the video, and then tell your world that you were sent back to your planet as the ultimate peacemakers. We the Soulfurian nation will be behind your every word, until this mission is over."

"We have been monitoring the buildup of nuclear weapons all over your planet. We are not happy about this as you know."

"We plan to eliminate every nuclear weapon from your planet. We need your help in doing this."

"We would rather see you talk to your leaders to dismantle them all, before we resort to executing, the other final plan."

"Other final plan?" Axel asked, in his telepathy communication.

"Well, the Soulfurian powers to be, took a vote on regeneration of Soulfuturans on your planet. We see how well it turned out from our first one, with the elimination of the Dinosaurs. We figure your human race will eventually eliminate life on your planet, and kill every Starsoul in the atmosphere, through nuclear war with absolutely no survivors."

"We figure if we bombard your planet with asteroids as we did in the past, we would end up with millions of survivors. The survivors would be trained by us to dismantle the weapons and surely keep the Soulfuturan life alive on your planet Earth."

"What is the Soulfuria nirvana event?" Tele-communicated Zhang.

"The one thing I didn't explain about Starsouls to you, is in the Starsoul laws video. The video that shows when the Star dies, it expands big enough to touch its planets and consumes them."

"When the time comes for the Stars heat to reach the planet's atmosphere, it causes the atmosphere to expand, and opens it up to the cosmos."

"Once that happens, all the Starsouls on the planet and in its atmosphere, escape to nirvana. The Starsouls may roam the universe in complete nirvana."

"You see, we have been planting Soulfurian Starsouls in Earth's atmosphere for future generations."

"We figure, we have about a hundred thousand years to the Soulfuria Nirvana event. We can leave Soulfuria, but there will still be billions left behind on Soulfuria to wait for nirvana."

"You're talking about wiping out our human race down to a few million. What makes you think we will help you do this?" tele-communicated Alexandre.

"Well, you don't have much of a choice if you want to see your human race survive. Your challenge will be to convince all the world's leaders to lay down their arms."

"They sent you to space to do this same exact thing. We are sending you back to take charge, and lead your fellow men, woman and child to world peace," the Soulfurian leader tele-communicated.

"What is the big plan on how we can achieve this, because I'll tell you the truth, they will just arrest us and throw us in jail, if we start telling them what to do?" tele-communicated Adam.

"When I told you, we would be there for you every step of the way I meant it."

"They will not arrest you, because although we are returning you to your planet, you will be taking over your International Space Station as your headquarters, and you will be calling the shots from there."

"Any spacecraft that tries to come to the station, will be met with a giant force field we will install around it, once it enters it. If they try to send a rocket to destroy the station, we will instantly deflect them away with lasers," tele-communicated the Soulfurian leader.

"What about the crew on the Space Station, what if they don't cooperate?" Tele-communicated Axel, the German astronaut.

"We do not condone violence to gain order, so we will surgically implant a microchip behind your ears, that will give us the ability to hear your conversations, and when we see fit, we can send our lasers to put the aggressor to sleep for a while. This tactic has its advantages to make someone cooperate without using force. You hardly even feel the implantation of the microchip. It is so small you will just feel a pin prick behind the ear," tele-communicated the Soulfurian.

"Ok, you preach keeping Starsouls balanced by keeping your actions good. You don't condone violence to gain control. Then how the hell can you justify threatening to wipe out billions of humans?" tele-communicated Jeremiah.

"That is a very good questions my peacemaker. Let's say a person goes hunting to kill deer, just for the sport of it. Then another one goes hunting to kill a deer to eat, and feed and clothe his family. Now which example is keeping their Starsoul balanced?" tele-communicated the Spangel.

"Well, of course, the latter of the two," replied Jeremiah.

"Exactly, when we make a sacrifice to eliminate a species as the dinosaur or the human race, we make the decision out of desperation, to keep our Soulfurian race alive. It's a matter of life and death of our species, and we have been around much longer than you."

"We have a bigger role to play in the cosmos. We will never harm a life for the fun or sport."

"We avoid violence at all cost. That is our intention on this mission, as you will find out."

"We have played this scenario over and over again, to where the calculated outcome is for ending this resolution, with none of your humans getting hurt."

"We cannot tell you the outcome, but have faith in us, and we have not deceived you up to this point in time. Like I said before, you really have no choice."

"Once we bring you back to the space station, there will be a lot of media fixed on the event. Let the initial celebration occur for a while, as you get ready to lock down the space station. Get on the media for the demand of world leaders to come to your attention. I want you to demand these leaders, to draw up a resolution to dismantle all weaponry of nuclear origin."

"At the same time, you are doing this, you must preach our Starsoul Laws, and demand the leaders of your great nations are in violation."

"We Soulfurians, will be sitting ready all along the asteroid belt in your galaxy. We will have one million spacecraft hovering, and just waiting to wreak havoc, with asteroid showers, wherever we may wish on the planet."

"This all sounds like a recipe for disaster. We all know that they will not believe our warnings, and they will just scoff at us. Then you are going to just hail down asteroids? That will make things worse. There will be an all-out Human- Soulfurian war, which the humans will come out on the short end of the stick. Why go through all of this, when we can foresee the outcome?" tele-communicated Maurice.

"You have to be positive in all of this. You cannot let your Starsoul become unbalanced, with doubt and regret. Work hard to win the hearts and minds, of your leaders and your people. Your leaders are very smart people. That is how they became leaders."

"They will know what's at stake and will heed confrontation with a force they don't understand."

"We have pinpoint locations of any human on your planet. We can temporary disable anyone instantly, with our laser capabilities. It doesn't matter if they are in a shelter or not. Our lasers have homing device technology. They will go around an object, or through a window, or ventilation pipe, or around the corner of any building to find their target."

"This is the power you will have, dealing with threats from your leaders. The world will see the power you have. Teach the Starsoul laws, no matter who opposes it. You may not be able to convince a person, but you will be able to disarm them," tele-communicated the Spangel.

"Ok, how exactly are we going to make the leaders sign a disarmament pact? What pull would we have in making that happen?" tele-communicated Jacques, the French astronaut.

"You simply will tell whatever world leader, that if they do not agree to disarm their nuclear stockpile, fireballs from the sky will reign down on them. We will listen to your conversations, and make it happen. Please don't abuse this power. Remember our main goal in all of this, is complete world peace on Planet Earth."

"We are now coming up on your Milky Way Galaxy. I will need all of you to go to the first level and prepare your departure from the spacecraft. Before we transport you to your space station, I need you all to line up to be inoculated, with our communication chip," tele-communicated the Spangel.

All the astronauts were eager to leave and get back to Earth. They all went to their sleeping quarters and collected their belongings. While they were getting ready, planet Earth was getting something also.

It was a response from the Soulfurian spaceship. Let's go down to Earth and listen in.

"We are sorry to interrupt your evening programming, to bring you this breaking story." "Good evening," this is Tom Cordeaux from the New York Evening News. There is breaking news coming in from Texas and Florida. There has been a response from the communication device built on the International Space Station. Let's go to Houston to get the story."

"Good evening, all you great citizens around the world. My name is Joseph C. Driver Jr. Thank you in advance for the opportunity to speak on behalf of N.A.S.A., and the International Space Community."

"Ever since the disappearance of our twelve young astronauts, that we have been calling our twelve angels. Who left this world in the name of world peace to better mankind? We have constructed a communication satellite, specially designed to send a never-ending signal out to the universe."

"The message we have transmitting is, "Bring Our Angels Home" in Morse code."

"Well, tonight people we have received not one, but one hundred messages back in the same Morse code, from the direction of the Galaxy Andromeda stating,

"We are returning your world's twelve peacemakers." These transmissions have been recorded and confirmed not to be a hoax or joke of any kind."

"This is a breakthrough in mankind's history. This is the first ever communications between humans and Extraterrestrials. These transmissions are the real deal. These transmissions are making world history.

People are dancing in the streets down here in Texas, and down there in Florida where the news originated."

"You heard it here first folks. Right here on W.N.Y.E.N. Evening News. They are coming home! Everyone here in the studio is hugging each other in relief. We feared the worst, and all our prayers are now answered. This is a great thing for the world."

"Let's go to Cindy Ancello, our news reporter. She is stationed at Time Square, and she has one hell of a crowd with her."

"Thanks Tom, Hello, this is Cindy Ancello, reporting here from Time Square here in New York City."

"Look at this crowd here, it is a sea of humanity, as more and more people are hearing the news. There are people walking around in alien costumes."

"Others wear E.T. Shirts, but one thing is common amongst all people, is that everyone is in celebration. The city is alive with celebration."

"We are entering a new age, an age where we can communicate with aliens. This is a great time to be alive, and the people here are demonstrating it. Let's switch back to you Tom. This is Cindy Ancello, signing out at Time Square."

"Ok, Cindy don't get hurt down there, be careful. All right now, we just received word that the President of the United States, is about to make a Presidential Address to the nation, from the Capitol in Washington D.C. Let's listen in."

"Ladies and Gentlemen, the President of the United States!" "Good evening fellow Americans. What a pleasant night it truly is. I am proud to bring you the great news, that our angels / astronauts, are alive." "It has been one year since the tragic day of their disappearance. We have been waiting for this news, on a glimmer of hope from our buddy's at N.A.S.A. They put up this communication device and pointed it at the stars. Well today my friends, the stars came back shining."

"Ringing in the news the alien entity is bringing them back. This is the first contact we had with actual life outside our universe. The messages came back in Morse code, so that's one thing we have in common."

"We might build a long-term relationship from that."

Then the president chuckled, apparently the message that came back from the cosmos, was generated from the Andromeda galaxy and read, "We are returning your world's twelve peacemakers."

"I'm guessing the astronauts explained to them what their mission was, in order for them to call them peacemakers. Anyway, this is the best news we have heard since their disappearance. We are working closely with the other world leaders on a reception party for them. We are working out details as we speak."

"I will be fielding questions, while I wait for the next briefing from my cabinet."

The gentleman in the front here, you can go first." "Mr. President my name is Todd Fairman, of course this is a great time in history, but does this open new door, as far as alien life belief?"

"Good question Todd, my educated answer to that, without upsetting any faiths, alien life can fall under God created them too. I am just hoping for a safe return of our astronauts."

"Young lady on the right your next: "Hello Mr. President, my name is Shirley McCallion, and my question is, how do you handle, or what is the procedure for bringing twelve astronauts back from alien captivity? I imagine they will be put under a microscope for investigative purposes."

"Well, I would not say quite that, but there are seven nations involved here, and each one has their own agendas on these astronauts. Yes, after a year with these aliens, the astronauts will be very helpful in our understanding of such aliens." "Whenever our astronauts are on long extended missions, they automatically go through ten-day quarantines. The reasoning for this quarantine will be to make sure they are not introducing any alien germs, or diseases to our planet."

"I will field one more question, then I will have a departing announcement to make."

"The young man on the left with the blue shirt on, it's your turn."

"Good evening Mr. President. My name is Michael Cordon, dealing with these aliens, are we going to just let them go with no altercations, after holding our astronauts for a year? Don't you think we should send them off with a bang, so they never come back, and show the human race is a race not to be messed with?"

President: "We would like to hold our options open at this point. We are entering waters we never tread before. Our first priority is to get our astronauts home, and then we can focus on the alien situation. We don't have weaponry to use in space, so our options are limited. Like I said, we will just settle to get our astronauts home safely."

"Ok before I leave you tonight. I just received word we have picked up the alien spacecraft, and it is headed to the International Space Station."

"All the seven nation leaders met with my cabinet, and we are all flying military personnel to the space station, to pick up the astronauts. Stay tuned to your local news for up to date information. Goodnight."

"Let the Games Begin"

The astronauts made their way to the lower deck getting ready for departure.

Eve looked at all the guys, and tele-communicated, "Well, we traveled so far to find peace for our nation. Let's stick together until the end, and carry on as real leaders, to bring peace to our world. With the help of these Soulfurians, I think we can pull it off.

If we could get the message of Starsouls across to the people, and they find out that they only need to lead a non-violent humble life. By keeping their Starsouls balanced, they will not fear when their natural life ends, and their bodies perish. If we could successfully convey the message, and gain world peace, then we will accomplish what we were sent in space to do. Does anybody disagree or do we all stand together?"

The other eleven astronauts slowly closed in on Eve until you could not see her anymore, and all raised their hands that met overhead in solidarity. "We are the new world order!" The Russian astronaut communicated.

Just then a Soulfurian came to the crew to administer their communication chip inoculations behind their earlobes. After the procedures were finished, the lead Soulfurian appeared on the lower level to give the astronauts instructions, while they were dressing in their N.A.S.A. space suits.

"Hello, my peacemakers," the Spangel tele-communicated. "The time is soon for the return to your world. You must stand strong in your mission. We have communicated with your world, letting them know you were returning. We have picked up transmissions, that your military is tracking us for your return. We expect your military to be present for your arrival. We already set a magnetic force field around the International Space Station.

"When they arrive with their space cruisers, the force field will repel them away. The force field will not affect our spacecraft. The communication chips you all received will disintegrate on our command, after this mission. Your telepathy ability will stay with you the rest of your lives. You will find out there are other human beings, that we call Soulfuturans that have developed this ability in the general public. So be on guard of what you are thinking when in public."

"Each one of you will be given this Soulfurian video chip as a gift from us to spread the word of Starsouls. Display this video to justify your demands from your leaders for peace. I will need you to call on all leaders in control of nuclear weapons. I will need you to demand for them to sign the Nuclear Disarmament Accord, N.D.A. for short. After seeing the video, some will sign with no contest."

"Meanwhile, back on Earth the whole world is tuned into their local T.V. stations, for an emergency briefing from the Pentagon, by The U.S. President."

"Ladies and Gentlemen let's welcome the President of the United States."

"Good evening fellow Americans, I would like to start off with a big "Thank God." Our angels are coming home. Yes, we have the Alien spacecraft, locked in our radar headed back towards. We don't know exactly what will happen when they arrive."

"I have called on Chief Commander of our U.S. Air Force Space Defense Division to lead this campaign."

"His name is John A. Leonard. He will call the shots of this historic event, live on your television screen. We have a live feed from our Air Force Military Command center, at MacDonald Air Force Base, in Tampa, Florida, and the International Space Station for the astronaut's arrival. I will head back to headquarters and be in communication with all the world leaders on this historic evening."

"I will break away now and let the media focus on Commander Leonard from this point on."

"Welcome fellow Americans, I am Chief Commander John A. Leonard of the United States Air Force Space Defense Division. Please excuse me as I always wanted to say that to a national audience. I've practiced that a million times in the bathroom mirror at home in the past."

"I just let that one out there to put everyone in a good mood and relieve tensions in this historic event. As you know, we are tracking on radar this giant alien spaceship. Saying that, we are pretty confident that our fellow Astronauts, and our European astronauts are aboard that craft heading to Earth right now."

"Our Military is on the way to the International Space Station."

"We hope that is where they are being returned to. Our military is working in unison with seven other country's militaries to guide these astronauts, or should I refer to them, our national heroes back home."

"We have our state-of-the-art space fighter, equipped with two nuclear warheads, capable of blowing that spacecraft out of the cosmos if needed."

"Of course, we will show all restraint to this alien presence at all cost, to get the astronauts back safely."

Then the camera's focused to the International Space Station. Once again, all the world media was ready, and waiting at the same spot one year ago today, looking in outer space to see the alien spacecraft return. On the streets around the world, people were gathering at local areas, with outside video feeds, like Time Square in New York City.

Once again like a year ago, all the world leaders were in communication with each other, putting all the differences between them on the back burner for this united event.

The world was waiting, as Commander Leonard was communicating with his spaceflight crew, aboard the U.S. space jet defender.

"Commander, we are almost at the International Space Station, and we can already see the giant alien craft. It is headed to the space station."

"Ok," Commander Leonard replies. "Lock and load all arms and wait for my orders." "Yes sir," the lead crew member replied.

Just then the cameras shifted to the Space station, and low and behold, there it was. The biggest spacecraft anyone has ever seen. The crowds at Time Square were thrown back in awe, when it showed up on the giant screen.

The pro alien people were going crazy, with their alien costumes in the crowds. The seven nation countries leaders were going back and forth on the phones. All the world media cameras were focused on the alien spacecraft.

It was a giant circular black disc, with a glass bubble dome on the top, and all color lights spinning round on its outer edge.

A giant triangular concave indent was on the bottom side of the spaceship, with a bright blue light coming from the center. It was a spectacular sight for the entire world to see. The American space defender crew called to Commander Leonard and said, "We are here at the International space station, and so are the other seven countries' space jets, and we cannot board the landing strip. The alien spacecraft docked overhead, has some kind of a magnetic field, and it is blocking us from doing so. We have to just sit here and watch."

"This is the dawning of the Age of Aquarius," replied Commander Leonard. "This is one spectacular sight. Just sit back and keep an eye on these guys. We need to see our astronauts released safely before we can do anything from this point."

As the world watched, a giant flexible tube emerged from the bottom of the alien spacecraft and wiggled its way down to the loading deck of the International Space Station. The crowds around the world were watching, like it was a science fiction movie.

Back on the Soulfurian spaceship, the astronaut crew was ready to depart the spacecraft, and return to their world as the new world leaders. They were all in agreement, this was the best opportunity to bring their world to peace, and they will stick together, until the mission is accomplished.

"We will do what is needed for this mission to come out peaceful," tele-communicated by Maurice.

Just at that point the astronauts, one by one, saluted the Spangel and were handed a digital circuit chip by the Lead Soulfurian.

They then were led down a narrow hall with glass windows on the sides. It seems to be a long hallway with an exit door at the end.

As the astronauts were going down this long hallway, there were Soulfurian crew members on the other side of the glass windows, watching them parade by in their N.A.S.A. space suits.

"Look here," Adam tele-communicated to the rest. "We have an audience sending us off. We won't let you down" Adam yelled, as he was the first to the exit door. He opened the door and stepped into a black tube and disappeared.

The other eleven followed behind Adam, as they all one by one entered the exit and disappeared. As the world cameras watched, they saw the first astronaut come out of the black flexible tube, and land safely on the International Space Station deck.

After the first another followed, and then another, and another, until all twelve were standing on the International Space Station deck in their N.A.S.A. spacesuits. The whole world was cheering, it was a wonderful sight.

There was a sense of compassion with the live public toward the alien spacecraft, as they were releasing the astronauts. Adam, and the others were standing there on the deck, they looked back up at the alien spacecraft hovering overhead and could see the other eight human star jet fighters being kept at bay, by the alien's magnetic field. Just then, Maurice heard a voice in his head. It was the Spangel talking to him through telepathy from the spacecraft.

Maurice tele-communicated to the others, "Please be quiet, the Spangel is giving directions."

So, it was like slow motion, all the astronauts bouncing up and down on the international Space

Station deck, with an alien spacecraft overhead, and eight human jet fighters surrounding the alien craft.

"Maurice, this is the leader of the Soulfurian Starfleet Federation. The lead Soulfurian asked me to take over this mission. I am an expert in troubled situations, and I need all of you to enter your Space Station and stay inside."

"We are being threatened with hostility by these human space jet fighters, and we need to neutralize the situation."

"Ok" said Maurice, as he directed all the astronauts inside the space station. They entered one by one. They were met by members of the Space Station. They were being scanned by Geiger counters for radiation.

"Hello astronauts and welcome home, I am Sergeant Harvey S. Simmons, I will be briefing you on your return to humanity. I know you all must be delirious from alien captivity, and probably need food and water."

"Before we go ahead and prepare all of you for decontamination and ten-day quarantine, here on the space station, there is a whole world that wants to hear what you have to say." "After your interview with the media, you will report to the decontamination quarters."

'Also, during this interview, you will give no information on your experience on the alien spacecraft."

"This is being deemed confidential, and classified information to the entire world militaries. Also, you may face court-martial for violating the restriction."

"You will simply say you have no memory, or they brainwashed your memory."

Eve was enraged immediately; of the controlling treatment the peacemaking astronauts were getting after being away for a year. The rest of the astronauts were also upset of the verbiage coming from Sergeant Harvey Simmons.

Meanwhile back on Earth at the United States Air Force Space Defense division headquarters in

Florida, Chief Commander John Leonard was in communication with his crew on the space jet fighter, when the whole world heard him say, "Get ready to fire on the alien spacecraft." The masses watched in horror as five eight jet fighters fired their nuclear ballistic missiles at the alien spacecraft.

The whole world was watching the alien spaceship being attacked. There was this strange blue glow that formed over, and around the alien spaceship just as the missiles were about to hit.

The blue glow was another magnetic field that deflected all five missiles into outer space, and away from the alien spacecraft. The masses of humans on Earth watching, erupted in cheer for the alien spacecraft. I guess it was human nature rooting for the underdog. Then they saw Chief Commander Leonard instruct his crew back to Earth, fearing the aliens would retaliate on the defenseless space jets.

All the other countries also pulled the plug on this hostile attack and ordered their space jets to return to Earth also. The astronauts and the crew on the

International Space Station did not understand what the world just witnessed, outside above their heads in space.

The leader of the Soulfurian Starfleet federation communicated with Maurice after that exchange, and tele-communicated to him, "The mission has begun, I will need your astronaut crew to take over the space station."

"We will temporarily knockout the Medias satellite feeds until you have total control. We will assist you in this matter and subdue your resisters without violence."

Maurice immediately briefed his astronaut crew and ordered the space station crew around. Anyone that would argue with them would be mysteriously put to sleep by the alien lasers, coming from above. Once asleep the astronauts would restrain them to captivity.

Sergeant Harvey Simmons was the first to be subdued and tied up.

This power takeover on the space station took about a half an hour to complete. Most of the operational crew complied with the astronaut's direction, after they seen what would happen, if they didn't agree.

Maurice then called up to the Soulfurian Starfleet leader, and tele-communicated to him their progress, and that the space station was secure.

The Soulfurian tele-communicated to Maurice and said, "Ok, now that you have the Space station secure, and after we sent the human space fighters' home, we can begin your world peace mission, and our Soulfurian regeneration mission."

"Once both missions are complete, we will both be able to see our species thrive, until one day we all become one. I will need you and your crew to be firm, and not to give into any negotiation, until all world leaders signatures are on the Nuclear Disarmament Accord, N.D.A. for short."

"We will reconnect transmissions with your world, and let you handle things the way you have to. We will be letting you know if we have to force asteroid strikes, and when, and where they will happen. Let's now get this mission completed."

Maurice then looked at his eleven comrades and tele-communicated, "Is everyone ready to do this?"

The other astronauts all gave Maurice a big thumbs up. It was time for the astronauts to shine.

All the astronauts went into the conference room, and took their seats at the long table, set up with twelve seats and twelve microphones. The camera lights came on, and the video screen came alive in the room up on the wall.

A grey-haired gentleman appeared on the screen and said, "Welcome home our twelve heroes."

"The world is watching you right now."

"I am Commander John A Leonard of the United States Air Force Space Defense division, here to give you a short interview, so you can get ready for quarantine, and official briefings. Can you all identify yourselves to the world, so they can relate to who you are? Just introduce yourselves one by one starting from left to right."

"The New World Order"

Adam started off the introduction with "What a long strange trip it's been" to the Grateful Dead's tune. That broke the silence and started off the rest of the introductions in a good sense and mood. You could see Adam was back to Earth, with his sense of humor. All the Astronauts were introducing their selves to the world audience.

The cameras and lights were flashing. As soon as the last astronaut was finishing his introduction, Chief Commander Leonard cut the German off, and interrupted saying. "Well, now the world knows you all are safe and sound, we will let you go to enter quarantine, and briefings by your government agents."

"Can you put Sergeant Harvey Simmons on the video feed, please?"

That's when Maurice took the microphone and said, "We have Sergeant Harvey Simmons subdued in the back-Commander Leonard, as we just took command of the whole International Space Station."

"You are out of line! Screamed Commander Leonard.

"I want to see Sergeant Simmons at once." Just then a laser came down from the Soulfurian spacecraft and put the Commander asleep. The world reactions were nothing but joyous, as they were cheering in the streets. Maurice then told the world that the twelve-person astronaut crew is the current, "New World Order."

Just then a lot of big wig politicians in Florida, Houston, and Washington DC., scrambled to find out what was going on. Other world military leaders were just as upset by the words of the astronaut. By a strange twist, the astronauts had a live audio, and video feed to every media outlet in the world, and the world media was eating up this story.

All over, every news station, and every headline in the papers it read, "Astronauts come back as New World Order."

"We Are the New World Order" claimed Maurice, once again to the cameras. It echoed all over the world.

"We are calling on all the world leaders to a summit. We have demands for them. They must comply with our demands. If they don't comply, the world will end as we know it."

The crowds stepped back as they were confused at the message. There was nothing anyone on Earth could do. The astronauts were on every TV around the world, with their demands. The United States Chief of Staff in Washington, Mr. Howard F. Bacon, stepped up to the microphone. He spoke to the astronauts.

"Where are these demands for world leaders to come to your attention coming from, Mission Commander Maurice?"

"The Soulfurians" was Maurice's reply.

"Soulfurians, is that the name of the aliens that held you captive? Are you being forced by them to make these demands?" questioned Mr. Bacon.

Jeremiah answered, "They are the ones that showed us the way."

"The way?" questioned Mr. Bacon.

"The way to world peace, and to show humanity how to live in total peace," replied Adam.

"They are out there waiting," Eve told Mr. Bacon. "They are waiting for us to take control of a few bad Starsouls that are threatening billions."

"Starsouls?" questioned Mr. Bacon.

"Yes Starsouls, they are the reason we are here," said Mr. Charles Jones the English astronaut.

"We are here to teach the world the meaning of Starsouls, which is life itself, and rid the world from evil, and eliminate every nuclear weapon on this planet," said Alex the German Astronaut.

"That's a mighty tall order you are asking, Mr. Bacon replied.

"Yes, and we will get it, in the name of humanity," said Malone the American astronaut.

"Ok, it is getting late, and I'm sure you guys are getting tired, after all you have been through. Let's give some time for things to settle down and let me meet with the President of the United States and go over with him these ridicules demands."

"Let's continue this conversation in the morning. It has been a great day today getting all of you back unharmed. We are still a little leery of an alien spacecraft, docked just above our Earth overnight."

'If we can get assurance from you, they are not here to harm us, I can get the President to negotiate with you in the morning."

Maurice speaks, "We demand all the world leaders to be in attendance at twelve noon tomorrow. This is when we will give them options to comply with our demands. At eight o' clock tomorrow morning we will come back on the air and tell the world the journey we have been on in the last year, and give them the Starsoul laws to live by, that the aliens showed us."

The aliens are called Soulfurians, and they are here to make sure we complete the peace mission, you guys sent us up here to do a year ago. They are our Space Angels, and you could consider them yours too. We will explain the details in the morning."

"Ok, that sounds like a plan. Let this meeting continue in the morning.'

"We will sign off and wish you all up there on the International Space Station a good night," said Mr. Bacon.

"Goodnight," said the twelve-person astronaut crew, as the transmission scrambled out and faded away.

The world was in awe of what just happened, as they walk home with their love ones with a lot of questions of what lies ahead. Although the astronauts seem brainwashed by the aliens, the general public likes what they are saying, and don't feel threatened by their demands.

The world leaders have all views of things. They are all scrambling, and calling each other, as we speak on their options, and their interest. The President called an emergency meeting of his Joint Chiefs of Staff, which is a body of senior uniformed leaders.

They are from the United States Department of Defense, who advise the Secretary of Defense, the Homeland Security Council, the National Security Council, and the President of the United States, on military matters.

They are meeting in the Oval Office, with the President. Let's listen in, as the meeting starts.

"Mr. President we have to stop meeting like this," said the Secretary of the Air Force.

"Let's face it, we all have been waiting for this day to come," said the Secretary of the Army.

"Well, we didn't exactly roll out the welcome mat to these aliens now did we?" asked the Secretary of the Navy.

"No, not exactly, they sent us home with our tail between our legs," exclaimed the Chairman of the Joint Chiefs of staff.

The President looks at the sixteen military leaders and says, "I have been on the phone with just about every world leader for the past few hours."

"Between them and all of us, we must extract those astronauts away from that space station, and alien presence. We simply have no defense for fighting an alien force, which is better equipped, and more technologically advanced."

"The world is looking to us, to lead the way to a solution. We must stay here all night if we have to, to take the media attention away from the astronauts without making the aliens mad." The Chairman replies, "We must keep everything calm tomorrow morning. We cannot cut the media feed to the astronauts, or the world public will be outraged."

"These astronauts are world heroes to the people. We cannot take away their voice."

"I agree," said the Army leader. "All this new world order shit, are the astronauts being put up to say this by the aliens?" "I believe they are brainwashed, and we can only wait to see what the aliens are up to."

"I agree," said the Navy leader. We need to ready all our military, and all our rockets that can reach space.

"We pass the instruction to our world neighbors and wait."

"We react after they act. Look at what happened to Mr. Leonard, do you think they will attack us with lasers like they did him?" asked the Air force leader.

The President left the room to take a phone call from the Chinese Emperor. The Chairman said to the Air force leader, "If they do, we better have our nightcaps on because all they did to Mr. Leonard was to put him asleep.

On a more serious note, does the Air force have the firepower to launch an attack on the aliens?"

The Air force leader replied, "They have a magnetic force field around them and the space station. If we can neutralize or disable the force field, then we have enough fire power to blow them back to the future." Everyone in the room chuckled. The President came back in. It looked like he had something to say.

"Gentlemen, I just got off the phone with the Chinese Emperor, and he told me he was in a conference with the Pakistani and Indian Leaders.

All three conferred to the decision, to wait till morning to see what the astronauts had to say."

"Also, remember what the American astronaut Maurice called the aliens, and cautioned that they could be our space angels too."

"If that statement is true, why would we want to harm a space angel?" After that news from the President, all the Chiefs of Staff agreed mumbled to each other and came to a decision to call it a night until the morning.

"Revelation"

Its six thirty A.M. the next morning, as the world is awaking to a new era. There are cars with loudspeakers in the streets waking everyone up, announcing to them to go to the arenas, stadiums and theaters, for the live viewing of "The New World Order."

The world's audiences are gathering in droves, to anywhere there is a public video screen with a live news feed. It is a scene in biblical proportions, as they gather for the event, they will find out to be the new revelation.

There are stadiums all over the world with seating for hundreds of thousands in each, just filling up with humanity. It is slowly happening. The world for this time is at peace, all working in unison to gather together to see what the astronauts, and aliens have in store for them. It is an event bigger than any event in history.

The entire world has faith in these twelve astronauts, after knowing they spent a year in the company of extraterrestrials and returned to tell their story.

This was better than any novel they dreamed of reading. Mothers were holding their children's hands, as they gather to the stadiums. There was no need for police, or crowd control that morning, because everyone's minds were fixed on hearing from the astronauts. Just the fact that the astronauts wanted to sit down, and talk to the people, before they were to address their leaders, empowered the astronauts.

There were chants of New World Order, traveling through the world's crowds. There were also chants of Revelation. It was clear, the world's masses wanted the astronauts to reveal what they went through, and what they had in store for them.

They were weary of war, fed up with fear, tired of poor, hungry for truth, sick of suffering, worn of struggle, they wanted rid of racism, to say goodbye to bigotry, this was their moment. They knew it.

The clock strikes eight O' clock a.m. Eastern Standard Time. Although it is morning for those in this time zone, people are gathered in the middle of the night halfway around the world. This is truly a worldwide event. The video screen transmissions go from scrambled to absolute crystal clear, showing the astronauts sitting at a long table above the Earth, at the International Space station.

Maurice starts off with "Good morning world, and for some good evening. Hello, world my name is Mission Commander Maurice J Kālu. I would like to thank you all for showing this world stands together. We are the same twelve astronauts, that all of you sent up in space one year ago for world peace."

"In the middle of that event, you watched us get abducted by extraterrestrials."

"Well as far as we are concerned, we were taken away, and showed the true answer to world peace. Our Soulfurian Space Angels showed us the light to human salvation. They showed us where we came from, why we are here, and where the human race is headed."

"The Soulfurians are upset with us because we elect, and put into political power, a very small percentage of us that is poised to ruin the entire world. They took us away so we could come back and show you how to refocus your minds to what life's priorities really are, and how to live by them in the name of world peace."

"All of our leaders, that small percentage of humans, that have ninety-nine-point nine percent of us fearing each other, would have you all believe that the Soulfurians have us brainwashed or something. Well, we are here to tell everyone that is not the case, and how enlightened we are."

"We are here to show you our experience with the Soulfurians in the past year. You wonder and ask yourselves, what are these aliens doing here? Why did they take us away? What do they want?"

"Let me start off by explaining who these aliens are. They call themselves Soulfurians, and they are from a planet called Soulfuria. They tell us their planet is billions of years older than ours, and they live light years away. They claim to be the first life formed in the cosmos. They say they are every living thing's keeper."

"They do this by controlling Starsouls. In a little bit, USN Lieutenant Mission Specialist, Eve S. McGovern will come on, and speak a little bit about" Starsouls."

"As a matter of fact, we have a special video made by the Soulfurians, and given to us to show all of you our journey with them, and why they are here."

"Now I will sign off and let each of the astronauts guide you through the video, starting off with USN, Lieutenant Mission Specialist Eve S McGovern."

"Hello world" Eve shouts with joy! The world responds with a jubilant celebration.

They are all glad to see Eve again. Eve then says, "It's good to be back home. Ok, let's talk about Starsouls. First I am going to push this little button."

Eve pressed the button. A big three-dimensional video screen appeared in front of the camera. It showed the view the astronauts had of Earth, when they were brought back to see it. The world was witnessing the world of Starsouls, all throughout planet Earth.

"Do you see those billions of ghostly images traveling all around our planet?" Eve asked.

"They are Starsouls! Aren't they cool? Everything living on this planet has one of these things energizing their bodies. Everyone believes they have a soul, now the Soulfurians tell us what that soul is made of."

"You see, The Soulfurians showed us Starsouls, and told us what they are. They say they are combined cosmic stardust energies, which are positively and negatively balanced. They told us they energize our bodies until we die, then they rejoin the atmosphere and help power it."

"Your Starsoul will travel free with no worry or pain powering the wind in total harmony. They also told us you must keep your Starsoul balanced throughout your life, because if you perish with a negatively imbalanced Starsoul, it doesn't join the rest of the cosmically balanced ones in the atmosphere. It travels to our Sun and becomes fuel for the Sun to burn. That's not fun. The bottom line is, what the Soulfurians are telling us, is to live an honest life, for you will never know when it will end."

"Here is "The Starsoul Instruction," the Soulfurians want us to live by." Just then on the video screen appeared and displayed the belief of Starsouls for the entire world to read.

"The Starsoul Instruction"

- The Starsoul is life.

- A Starsoul is the center of everything living.

- A Starsoul combines positive and negative cosmic renewable energy, made up of every mix of cosmic Star elements.

Your Starsoul is located in the center of your brain, in your pineal gland.

- The life of a Starsoul is infinite, until the Starsoul has a bigger negative composition, which makes it no longer cosmically balanced, and falls victim to the Star in that solar system, upon the death of the body.

- A Starsoul energizes your thoughts, your speech, your body movements, your heart and your brain.

- Your eyes are the eyes to your Starsoul.

- It is the driving force behind everything you do for your whole life.

- Everything that is alive is moved by energy and living thing energies are called Starsouls.

- Most people on the planet have one belief in common. It's the belief of the soul, which is the Starsoul.

- Your balanced Starsoul lives forever. It has so much energy, it wears out your body it occupies over time, and eventually takes on a new one, or just joins all the Starsouls powering the atmosphere.

- When a balanced Starsoul is not occupying a physical body, it is traveling the atmosphere in perfect freedom.

- Your physical body may perish, but when it does all the Starsoul energy releases from your body.

- Everything that is alive in this world is powered by a starsoul.

- If your Starsoul becomes corrupt and imbalanced with more negative energy at bodily death, it will be consumed by its Star.

- Your Starsoul is the driving force behind every growth of the body, and the direction the body takes in forming. The energy makes cells divide.

- A combination of an infinite number of Starsoul's energy, powers the atmosphere that circles the planet. They are very much the energy that moves the Gulfstream, powers the wind, and drives the waves in our oceans. They power thunderstorms, waterfalls and moves lava, hurricanes and tornados.

- All living things have Starsouls; D.N.A. makes up the structure of the body as the Starsoul powers the D.N.A. to form.

- "A newborn baby can have all the physical characteristics of the male and female, but its Starsoul is a one of a kind, unlike the male or female parents."

- "Every element that the human body contains is found to come from the Star, for us it is our Sun.

- A Starsoul energizes these elements. The Starsoul is the ultimate superconductor of energy for the body."

- Your Starsoul is doing your thinking for you, so if you are thinking negative or evil, then most likely your Starsoul is in a negative cosmic state.

- Every generation of humanity is smarter and more technically advanced than the past generation, due to newborns acquiring advanced civilization's cosmic Starsouls."

- • A negative thought or action is balanced by a positive thought or action, which balances a Starsoul.

- A Starsoul never leaves the planet's atmosphere, unless it is unbalanced once it leaves the body.

- A Starsoul will live on to roam the atmosphere until inhaled or absorbed by a fertile female.

- A Star consumes negative Starsouls, and produces cinder Starsoul dust, when its flares erupt and lash out

- The negative Starsoul dust from the Star bounces off its planet's atmospheres and is collected by its moons.

- The Moon is full of negative Starsoul dust, which makes the moon negative, pulling on the positive Starsoul atmosphere of the Earth, which causes the high and low tides.

- A Starsoul is a vital part of reproduction. When a fertile female absorbs a Starsoul through rain or snow falling on the skin or through inhalation, it resides in the unborn fetus and energizes the baby through life.

- Mother Nature is a combination of all Starsouls in the world.

- Every Star emits different Starsoul energies

- God is great, and God created everything in the universe, God created all galaxies, all of the Solar systems galaxies contain. God created the Stars that created Starsouls.

"The Teachings"

After the list had been read by the public, there was an outcry of Starsoul chants by the masses. In every country, in every state, in every city, and town you heard Starsouls! Starsouls! Starsouls! There were also chants of Space Angels! Space Angels! Space Angels! It was something the human race has never heard of. Everyone could instantly connect with the Starsoul in them.

It was something for the non-believers to believe in. It hit home with the human race because it made perfect sense to them. They wanted to hear more.

"Hello world, this is Flight Engineer Jeremiah D Edelman. It feels so good to be back home again."

The world gave Jeremiah a warm response. Jeremiah clicked the button to bring up the video screen again, of the astronauts getting sucked up through the giant vacuum tubes.

"Do you see when this happened? The vacuum pulled us up in a fast spiral, which spun us so hard it rendered us unconscious. Little did we know it ruptured a blood vessel in our brains. It sent blood flowing to a new section of our brains, that enabled us to communicate with each other through mental telepathy, isn't that cool?"

"We still can use it today, and we will use it for the rest of our lives. So now all of us astronauts, and Soulfurians can communicate with each other, through vast distances all the time. The Soulfurians told us that everyday humans in future generations will naturally develop this technology, as they keep acquiring Soulfurian Starsouls through the generations."

"If you look at the screen, you can see the planet Soulfuria. You can see all the Soulfurian Starsouls, surrounding their planet in their atmosphere. Cool, isn't it?"

The world's masses were in awe when they saw the giant Soulfurian planet.

"We were on that planet twice during our trip," exclaimed Jeremiah.

"By them showing us our planet with its Starsouls, and their planet with their Starsouls, they were telling us something, but we weren't picking up what they were trying to communicate just yet. We were just learning the purpose of Starsouls at the time."

"We had a good experience on the Planet Soulfuria, and they were the perfect host. It was a planet of order, and no violence, or evil could be sensed there."

Also, we got to order food rations from get this, a virtual three-dimensional video screen. Tell me if that isn't cool."

"Hello world, I'm back! I am N.A.S.A. Mission Specialist, Malone L. Akbar. It feels sooooooo good to be back."

The world welcomes Malone with open hearts. "Yea, they told us about Starsouls, and only the Soulfurians can see them."

"They told us that they are the keepers of Starsouls for all the galaxies. Then we questioned them about being Gods, and they scoffed at us, like comparing us to being Gods because of our test tube, and stem cell research technology."

"The Soulfurians told us they also were created by a God, who created the big bang. They told us the difference is, they were created billions of years before we were, and we were created by their tinkering of Starsouls."

"Sounds weird, but after leaving their planet, they took us on a ride through the cosmos. They took us to places you would only see in your dreams. This was an adventure, that one day, I might write a book on. I might call it "Starsouls."

"They took us to another Galaxy called The Carnherbivorous galaxy, as you can see in the video. In this Galaxy, they took us to these planets from millions of years ago, that are still thriving today."

"The first planet was called Reptilia. There was nothing but millions of different reptiles on this planet. There were thousands we couldn't even identify."

"You see, they told us when our planet was made, millions of years ago, the only Starsouls our Sun, or Star created, were plant and fish life Starsouls. Also, our world was just a giant greenhouse."

"That's when the Soulfurians started tinkering with different planet's Starsouls.

They took these reptile Starsouls and dropped them in our Earth's atmosphere, and after thousands of years of aquatic life reproducing with theses reptile Starsouls, the reptiles evolved and roam our planet for millions of years."

"Does everyone see the reptile Starsouls all over that planet? That's just the beginning of our trip. These Soulfurians are our friends, and do not wish us any harm."

"There is a reason they need us to thrive as humans, and they want nothing to happen to us. They compare our world to their proverbial fish." bowl."

"You know, how you can control a fishbowl environment by putting in whatever fish to live there, and what plants to live in that bowl, and can keep the water temperature just right."

"Well, you can only keep that fish tank world alive from the outside. You can never dive in the bowl to fix things, when they go wrong. This is how they take care of our world."

"They have been watching us since the beginning of time. Their likeness is drawn on ancient cave carvings, on Egyptian hieroglyphics, all throughout the ages in all countries, there are drawings of their likeness."

"They are the same aliens in Hollywood movies, since the beginning of stardom and TV."

"They are the same Soulfurians that crashed in the desert in Roswell that our leaders kept secret."

"They let us evolve, and thrive until the big piranhas, threaten our world from continuing."

"The big Piranhas they are referring to is, all world leaders with their fingers on the nuclear triggers."

"Howdy World, "The Duke is Back" Adam spoke in his "John Wayne" voiceover.

The world erupted with applause as Adam introduced himself.

"This is Major Tom reporting to Ground Control; your Texas Cowboy has landed!"

"Did you ever want a ride on an alien spacecraft all around the Cosmos? It crossed my mind as a Mission Specialist, but only in my wildest dreams.

"We spent most of our time on the top floor of the spaceship, and it had a dome of glass all around us. It felt like we were traveling through space at incredible speeds standing up. That was one hell of a ride."

"These Soulfurian cats are for real! They took us and showed us their world, then sent us back to tell you guys, to wise up and fly straight."

"Because that evil thinking, and evil actions, will get you a one-way ticket to hell."

"You see hell every day when you look to the sky at our Sun. We are made of Stardust, and only the Sun can consume an unbalanced Starsoul."

"So, after they took us to Reptilia, they took us to planet Triassica, and boy was that scary. There were some big plant-eating dinosaurs all over that planet.we couldn't even land the spaceship."

"Then they took us to a planet called Jurrasica, and you sure know what that was like when you watched that movie with the title ending in 'Park." Then Adam winked his eye and said, "Hint, Hint. "

"The point they were making to us was that different galaxies put out Solar systems with Stars that are unique and put out different Starsouls."

"This galaxy we were in, put out reptiles and dinosaurs of all kinds. We saw the Starsouls in each of these different planet's atmospheres."

"That was till they took us to a planet that looked a lot like primitive Earth and was called Primatourious. Primates roamed all over this planet. Some had tails, and they were very hairy like cats and dogs." "They were upright walking creatures, with arms and legs like us. This was about the time the Soulfurians found out that their planet Soulfuria was in danger, and their Soulfurian beings were in danger."

"Their Sun, or Star was starting to expand, which is the start of the death of a Star. Their nitrogen atmosphere was heating up, and also expanding, putting Soulfurians in danger."

"They needed to find a new planet for their Soulfurian kind. They picked Earth, which is now 78.09% nitrogen, 20.95% oxygen, 0.93% argon, and 0.039% other gas. A lot different from the time it was a greater percentage of oxygen."

"They calculated this decreasing of Oxygen and increasing of nitrogen when they chose planet Earth."

"They felt it was a perfect choice for their nitrogen breathing race. So they set a plan to eliminate the dinosaurs from our planet, and clear the atmosphere of dinosaur Starsouls. We all know how that happened then, with asteroids, volcanoes, and years of dust blocking sunlight."

"Well, the Soulfurians started all of that, with their lasers deflecting asteroids, from our asteroid belt around our Solar system, to reign down on our planet."

"Once all the dust cleared, and dinosaurs were gone after thousands of years, the planet was ripe for new species growth. This was when the Soulfurians started their 'Regeneration Plan," to transfer their race onto this planet."

"They took primate Starsouls from Primatourious, and put them in Earth's atmosphere."

"Still millions of mammal species survived the asteroid assault. These primate Starsouls would combine with these mammals and started the emergence of primates on our planet."

"Once primates were present on Earth, that's when the Soulfurians mixed, Soulfurian Starsouls in our atmosphere. "While Adam was explaining all of this, the world was watching the video in shock. They were finding out how deeply the Soulfurians were involved in planet Earth."

Adam continued on with, "After years of reproduction of Hominid generations, and with each generation acquiring Soulfurian Starsouls, it was making the evolution of man, at and enormous growth in knowledge and technology. They have been infusing knowledge into every one of us through their Starsouls."

"They took Hominids, which took thousands of years to light a fire, to Egyptian life building pyramids. The Soulfurian regeneration process is still going on today with every generation of humans born with Soulfurian Starsouls."

"Look how fast we are evolving in just the last one hundred years. We went from horse and buggy and telegraph communications, to spaceships and smart phones. Every baby born today is smarter than dad and mom's generation. They explained to us that they look at us as future Soulfurians, and not Humans."

"They compared us to what we look like today, with most of our body hair gone, compared to our Hominid ancestors that couldn't light a fire, to us eventually gaining the ability to communicate in telepathy, and not needing earlobes to hear each other talking, and our mouths shrinking for the same reason."

"They told us our ozone level would eventually disappear causing us to wear protective eye caps, and with all future communication involving keyboards, pads, tablets, and smart phones, the tips of our fingers would eventually evolve to grow fatter in size."

"That is when we will transform from, human to Soulfurian. That is when the future human will look like the alien today." The world was stunned with this revelation. At the same time relieved knowing that the Soulfurians were not there to harm them."

Just then Maurice grabbed the microphone, and announced it was nearing twelve noon, and the European astronauts were ready to meet with world leaders, on the demands of the Soulfurians. Also, the astronauts would push for permanent world peace on this planet.

Meanwhile during the morning hours while the American astronauts were conveying the Soulfurian message to the human race, the world's United Nations leaders were all meeting at the United Nations building in New York City. The general assembly, comprised of two hundred and fifty-seven world leaders, waiting to meet with the returning astronauts.

The President of the United States was at the podium ready to speak. "To all the great leaders of our world, I just want to say thanks for making it to this emergency world crisis meeting."

"I have spoken too many of you in the past couple of days, on the planning of this meeting."

"We have listened to what the astronauts were telling the public this morning, and I'm sure a lot of you disagree with what they are saying. It seems, by the reactions of the people around the world, they like what the astronauts are telling them."

"The astronauts are more popular to the masses than we are right now. As I discussed with other world leaders, we need to get the public back on our side, before we have any confrontation with the aliens, or their demands."

"Before we get started, can we get a vote in the house, on how many of you leaders believe what these astronauts are saying?" There were approximately two hundred hands of the two hundred fifty-seven leaders. Most hands were from leaders from smaller countries, and the ones that are war torn, and have no answer to peace in their nation. A statistic that none of the superpower nation leaders were proud of.

"The Soulfurian Ultimatum"

"Ok", the President says, "We have about half of this world including the leaders who are following the astronauts lead. Well, let me say something to those two hundred leaders."

"You could believe in this Starsoul way of thinking, but just remember those astronauts are puppets to the aliens, and they are brainwashed by these same aliens."

"So, if what you say you believe is true, and you agree with aliens that just landed on our doorstep, after a hundred thousand years. This is a preposterous way of thinking if you ask me."

"We need to meet with these astronauts, and hear what the alien demands are, and then set them straight, to let them know where we stand."

The time was twelve o' clock Noon, Eastern Standard Time. The giant video screen came alive in the United Nations general assembly of world leaders.

The world was also watching the showdown between their leaders, and the astronauts. It all started with the Russian astronaut with English translation speaking.

"Hello world, and the great leaders of this world. I am Cosmonaut Dmitri S. Federoff."

"I have seen most of you leaders leading us down the path of war, over and over again. Well, we are here today to tell you No More!   The entire world started cheering Dmitri! Dmitri! Dmitri!

The Russian President jumped up and yelled, "COSMONAUT, YOU ARE OUT OF LINE!"

Just then a laser beam came from the sky, down through the United Nations window, to the assembly room, and struck the Russian leader right in his head. The assembly was in shock.

The Russian leader simply fell asleep. Two leaders carried him out to a room where he could sleep it off.

The United States President stood up and grabbed the mic and said, "Ok we see how this conversation's going to go, so let's be civil here, or everybody will just be sleeping through this."

There were applauds throughout the public masses at what transpired on the opening statement from the Russian astronaut, and what the American president said afterwards.

"Yes, that is right, we have been sent to space one year ago, and we come back as world peace makers, thanks to our friends the Soulfurians," Dmitri stated.

"It took the Soulfurian's presence to bring all the world's leaders, into one place for a common cause."

"Every generation of humans born, acquires a Soulfurian Starsoul, and it makes that human smarter than its predecessor."

"I praise them for that. They are watching everything we are doing daily, and there are things they don't like."

"They can live with most, but there's one thing that scares their future existence. As you seen in the video, they are the keepers of all the Starsouls in this galaxy, and every galaxy in the cosmos."

"For the last hundred thousand years, they have been dumping Soulfurian Starsouls in our atmosphere, causing us to evolve from Hominids, to Homo sapiens, to Soulfuturans. As the Soulfurian leader put it, we are halfway between looking like a hairy Hominid, to halfway resembling the Soulfurians themselves.

When you look at a skull timeline of humans, there is a stark jump from ape skull, which changed little in 34 million years, to a human skull that changed in size and shape in one million years in the evolution scale. Soulfurian Starsouls are the answer."

"With all that time invested into our human race, the last thing they want to see, is the people in that room you are in, ruining our world, and poisoning our atmosphere of all Starsouls, with nuclear radiation."

"Yes, you heard me right, Nuclear Weapons! They are here to make us dismantle them forever."

The world was rejoicing in the streets, they were celebrating the fact, a single astronaut had so much courage to tell the world leaders where the aliens stand. Finally, a force that was not political, had the world leaders in check.

The Chinese Emperor took the microphone and questioned with English translation; "Well, how do these Soulfurians plan to enforce such a difficult task?"

"Nuclear Disarmament Accord, N.D.A. for short," stated Zhang K. Chen, the Chinese Cosmonaut.

"This is a document that will make the nuclear warfare playing field, even at zero."

The Chinese Emperor scratched his head and said, "If all of our superpowers agree to eliminate such weapons, that will leave us at the mercy of terrorism, this cannot be!"

"Well if you had regular yearly and emergency summits like the one today, you would be able to vote worldwide, with every nation leader on hand, and vote a decision to go into their country and take them away. The whole point of the N.D.A. is not to just rid the world of nukes." "It is a whole new way of enforcing world peace."

"If every nation leader can join together, and vote for funding world hunger, and vote against, as the Soulfurians would say, the unbalanced Starsouls of the world, then this would be one happy world to raise our children in."

Just then the world rumbled from every corner of the Earth, with humans jumping up and down, hugging each other with joy.

"You're living a fantasy astronaut! Tell those aliens to take a hike," yelled the English President.

The whole world was waiting, and sure enough the laser from space, found its way to the English leader's cranium, and put him fast asleep. The world was amused.

The President of the United States took the microphone and said, " Ok, enough of this, let's get to the point."

"If we all do not agree to sign this accord, what are the alien's plans for repercussions?"

Axel P. Klein, the German astronaut grabbed the microphone and said in English translation; "Their repercussions Mr. President?" Well, let's say there are one million Soulfurian spacecraft stationed all along the asteroid belt in our solar system."

"As soon as you take a vote and come up one vote short, they are going to use their laser technology to deflect asteroids at the Earth in apocalyptical style just like they did to wipe out the dinosaurs."

In his English translation, he concluded with, "I am sorry to bring the bad news." There was total silence all around the world. The world was not expecting the German Astronaut to say the word apocalyptical.

They thought the aliens were there not to harm them, and what they just heard was the opposite.

The boo's started slowly, and then gained strength throughout the world, until a loud echo of boos surrounded the world airwaves.

The world population was suddenly confused, about what the astronauts were describing the aliens to be. When listening to them this morning, they described them to be friendly, peaceful, and all for world peace.

Now they are hearing threats of world destruction. The world was now thinking the aliens had the astronauts brainwashed.

This was all the German Chancellor needed to hear. He grabbed the microphone and in English translation, warned the German astronaut and the aliens, they would not be threatened like this. He told the astronauts that humanity would not stand for such threats, while they were engaged in peaceful negotiations.

Astronaut Mr. Haruto L. Tanaka replied in English translation; "Pardon me Mr. Chancellor; the Soulfurians are not considering this a peaceful negotiation.

They are just laying out their final agenda, of deciding what is best for their Soulfurian future."

"If there is nuclear war by the hands of us humans, this will poison every Soulfurian/ Human Starsoul, currently in our atmosphere. This means the

Soulfurians would need to start over and find another world to transfer their Starsouls."

"They figure, with their calculations, if they end life as we know it, through asteroid and meteor bombardment, then the lesser of two evils would prevail. They could still keep life on this planet, going through millions of human survivors, and billions of Starsouls added to the impaled atmosphere."

"This would be the worst-case scenario for us humans, if the vote comes out without a one hundred percent agreement to disarm all nuclear weapons."

"All they want for our human race is world peace, without the weapons that can annihilate our world and theirs."

The Prime Minister of Canada takes the microphone, and in his English translation say,   "Ok we understand their logic on worst cases scenarios. Put yourself in our shoes for a minute and think about what the aliens are asking us to do."

'How do we know, if the only thing we have that can blow their spacecraft out of our solar system, is the very thing they are asking us to dismantle? How do we as humans, believe these Soulfurians as you call them, are truthful in their claims?"

The Canadian astronaut grabbed the microphone. In an English translation replied with, "Mr. Prime Minister, with all due respect to you and all the world, if you believe in the Starsoul logic, and you watch the video of our trip, it's simple to figure out that the Soulfurians do not consider us Humans."

"They consider us Soulfuturans. They look at us as if we are their future ancestors."

"They designed us that way through the manipulation of Starsouls, and in each one of us they see one thing, and that one thing is a Starsoul."

"They consider if you have bad intent, as in stockpiling nuclear weapons, then you have an unbalanced Starsoul. They feel if the ninety nine percent of balanced Starsouls cannot stop the one percent with their fingers on the nuclear trigger, then they will have to step in and balance our Starsoul world."

The President of the United States takes the microphone and replies with, "Ok, we pretty much heard both sides of the situation at hand. We are going to have to vote on this decision to sign the N.D.A. Two questions we do have, if we come back in agreement across the board, will the aliens leave our world?"

"Also, what happens if one of us reneges on our end of the agreement, and strays away by stockpiling them again, will that decision ruin it for all of us?"

The French astronaut replied in English translation; "The Soulfurians heard your question, and they are happy that the question is based on an agreement, and they congratulate you in asking this question."

"They said to me for six million years they have done nothing to interfere with our evolution, and once they set the process in place, they have monitored our fighting and our wars throughout the centuries, and never interfered."

There was never a time in Soulfuturan history, they felt their future existence was threatened. They are the keepers of Starsouls throughout the cosmos. They have too big of a responsibility to the cosmos, to be hanging around our world. So, to answer your questions directly, once our race will live in a non-nuclear state, then they no longer are concerned."

"As for the second part of your question, that is also a valid question. They are telling me if you keep an open forum, and you have unified meetings at your United Nations building, then you will see the ones that stop attending. It will build your suspicions, along with your current technology of detecting a nuclear buildup."

"They are sure you will know how to handle it, and that the twelve of us will always have communication with the Soulfurians, if in case they are ever needed to be called again."

"They are constantly monitoring our progress, and they told me to tell you that they have heard all the Abbot and Costello episodes through radio waves."

They said that we are the loudest Starsouls in the universe, and we can keep no secrets.

With that statement, the United Nations leaders adjourned for a very important meeting. The astronauts also adjourned, as the video transmission went blank.

The astronauts were regrouping to get more instruction from the Soulfurians. It was an emotional rollercoaster day for the world masses. Starting off with emotional highs, after listening to the astronauts in the morning.

And then emotional lows, when hearing what the Soulfurians planned to do, if their leaders did not comply with their demands.

Then they finished the day with a lot of questions, about their governments intentions with their fate, once again in their hands.They were seeing a safe world being optioned to them, but also seeing what might happen if their leaders don't comply.

With that in everyone's mind, there was only one thing that did start mass demonstrations at each country's National Capitols, and government embassies, and government buildings.

"Humanity Looks to Find the Answer"

Millions were massed at Tiananmen Square, Time Square, and Parliament Square, with gathering places in every country around the world. They were all conveying the same message, "Give up the Nukes," "Sign the Accord." Every embassy and government building was overwhelmed with protesters. They were shouting, "Believe in the Starsoul."

There were people running and protesting in every country, city, and town in the world. It was chaos in the streets of New York. There were people wearing alien suits, with signs reading "Starsouls." No one in the world had any idea about their future. There were a lot of rumors spreading about aliens taking the world over. There was a general sense of it being the last days of human life. People were running to their local government buildings looking for answers.

The media was in a frenzy, to get coverage of the alien presence at the International Space station, and at the asteroid belt. They were hunting down local astrometry observation centers, to get a glimpse of the aliens.

The evening newspaper headlines read, "Is This the Beginning of the End Days?" "Will the Sky Rain Fireballs?"

Adam was back at the Space Station with Maurice, and the other ten astronauts. They were all communicating with each other, at a long meeting table using telepathy.

The Russian cosmonaut Dmitri tele-communicated with, "Boy, we are between a rock and a hard place, relaying the Soulfurian message to all the leaders. Do you think they will imprison us, if we ever get back to Earth?"

Maurice tele-communicated with, "I don't think so, whatever happens, if we have a planet to go back to, will be a different world, one way or the other."

"I get the Soulfurians will always watch over our shoulders if we live. With a backup like that, hell, they may even make us the future world leaders."

Adam called out to the Soulfurian leader, and the Soulfurian leader tele-communicated back quickly.

"Yes Soulfuturan, how may I be assistive to you?"

Adam tele-communicated, "I was wondering, after showing the world our experience traveling the cosmos, and them seeing Starsouls in the video, is there any way there is a possibility of showing the world, and our leaders, with their own eyes, Starsouls in our atmosphere?"

"Very good question my Soulfuturan, it seems your human mind is starting to think like a true Soulfurian. We already have in place a plan to do such a show of truth".

"We are waiting for the outcome of your leader's vote, on signing the accord. We are saving that show as one last option to convince unsigned leaders, that the only way to survive a peaceful world is to believe in the Starsoul."

Eve then questions the Soulfurian leader by tele-communication, "Will we have a chance to say goodbye to our loved ones back home, if the leaders refuse to sign the accord?"

The Soulfurian leader tele-communicated with, "The answer to that question will be up to the individual country leaders that refuse to sign. You must understand this world you call Earth, is a last-ditch effort to extend the existence of Soulfuria."

"Billions of Soulfurian souls will meet their nirvana naturally as our Star dies, but this planet is our future, and we will go to any length in making this happen. My advice to all of humanity at this point, is to make sure their Starsouls are balanced."

Meanwhile, back at the United Nations, the world leaders were once in session again to debate this ultimate decision. The U.S. President was once again conducting a poll on who was for signing the accord, and as the hands rose it appeared, they would have this thing signed quickly.

There were only nine hands not raised yet, and the U.S. President was one. Some also noted that all nine hands were from the only countries that possess nuclear weapons.

The President continues, "I see mostly all of you want to sign this accord. By my nation's laws read, in a democracy, the majority rules."

"If this were the United States decision, this would be a done deal. Sorry to say this is not a U.S. decision, it is a world superpower decision."

"The Nuclear superpowers, with the bad publicity we get on the nuke situation, there is a certain responsibility we have protecting our nations, and the world."

"What I am getting at is, it has been confirmed by our countries space observatories that there are millions of alien spacecraft hovering around the asteroid belt."

"We know they threaten to wipe us out with asteroids, like the dinosaurs were wiped out."

"But what if they were not telling us the truth, and want us to dismantle the only weapons we have, to defend ourselves against an all-out alien attack?"

The South African leader stepped up to the podium and addressed the U.S. President. He said,

"Mr. President, with all due respect to your world protection theory, we are a country that developed nuclear weapons, and dismantled them in a step towards world peace."

"We have no defense against an all-out asteroid or alien attack. Let's go back and look at this whole story from the beginning."

"These aliens showed up when our astronauts stepped into space looking for world peace."

"Then they took our astronauts on a history tour to show them their world, and our world, and how we both connect through Starsouls, the whole time never harming the astronauts. Then we put a signal out to bring them back, low and behold they returned them with a message to drop your arms, then open your mind to world peace through the belief of Starsouls."

"What happened then?" "We welcomed them by firing nuclear weapons at them, which they just shrugged off, like it was nothing."

"Now tell me Mr. President, those nuclear weapons you are holding to defend the world, what exactly will they do?"

The Israeli Leader stepped up to the microphone and replied to the question the South African President asked.

"With all due respect, we applaud your action in disassembling your nuclear weapon, in nineteen ninety-one. Now we are in the twenty-first century, and our enemies are bigger than ever."

"You may think that our nuclear weapons are useless on their spacecraft, and you may be right."

"I think we will keep our nukes for a different reason, and not for targeting alien spacecraft, but to defend at asteroids, that come hurling down on our planet."

"Even if we sign the agreement, how do we know if they will not just hang around until we have them dismantled, and then hurl these asteroids at us?"

"What will we use to defend ourselves against that type of attack?"

The Canadian Prime Minister stepped to the microphone, and replied to the Israeli leader, "People, do we realize what we are debating here? Does anyone look at the media, and see the masses demonstrating to lay down the arms. People, do you want to see the human race survive?"

"You, Mr. President, said yourself, millions of alien spacecraft are just waiting for us out there. Millions in the streets pray for you to lay down the nukes. Why in the world would you risk the lives of billions for these weapons?"

"Look, whether we have nukes or not, it is pretty obvious they could wipe us out. If you lay down your nukes, and everyone signs the accord, and they still attack us or destroy us, then they would be guilty of having unbalanced Starsouls, like they claim we should not live by."

"Why would they risk perishing in battle with their Starsouls unbalanced? I believe them, I believe in my Starsoul, and I truly believe they are Spangels."

"Spangels that kill" exclaimed the English Leader. "With all the third world countries trying to get their hands-on nuclear weapons it would be suicide to eliminate them, and we will do this on a threat from an alien race?"

"I say we toss a couple ICBMS at their asses and see if their magnetic shields can hold up to a force of one point two million tons of TNT."

"I say us nuclear countries form a pack to stick together and ride this out, countering any alien attack with whatever ICBMS we have in stock for deployment. My great nation and I will not be bullied around by a bunch of E.T.s."

After hearing the statement from the English leader, the Indian and Pakistan leaders both with nuclear capabilities stood at the podium. They bowed out of the nuclear alliance with a statement saying,

" We do not believe in attack; we have our nuclear weapons for defensive purpose only. If we are attacked, that will be the only time we would use them. What the Aliens and astronauts are conveying about

Starsouls, it is not too off of what we believe of the soul."

"We elect to stand by our people and the astronauts, and with full compliance, sign The Nuclear Disarmament Accord."

"Is there anyone else?" the President of the United States asked.

The Chinese Leader stepped up and said, "The Peoples Republic of China will join our friends, and also fall into compliance with signing the accord."

"But if attacked or provoked by anyone or anything, we will hold the right to defend ourselves."

"Ok, that is three countries out of nine that will agree to a total dismantlement of nuclear weapons, by signing the alien Nuclear Disarmament Accord."

After news of the count had leaked out of the United Nations meeting assembly, it reached the media, and was broadcast to the masses. It sparked chaos in New York City, the United Nations buildings was under siege.

The US military was deployed, and the Mayor declared the city under Marshall Law.

He warned anyone trying to enter the United Nation building, not being cleared by the military, would be shot on site.

Armed Apache helicopters were flying over the city. The whole area of the city around the United Nations building was barricaded off with rolls of ten-foot barbed wire.

The leaders of the world were in a military lockdown for their protection from the wild crowds, and anyone trying to make a heroin assassination attempt on any of the non-complying leaders, as in the US President or the English leader.

The news was transmitted to the astronauts at the international space station. The video feed from the space station appeared to be transmitting once again, and all the astronauts were visible on the screen, and every screen in New York City, also around the world.

Maurice, the U.S. astronaut starts off the video feed with, "The Soulfurians hear through TV transmissions in space that we have a decision from all the great leaders of our world."

"They also hear it is not a one hundred percent agreement to sign the Nuclear Disarmament Accord. Is that correct Mr. President?"

The President of The United States takes the microphone and answers," Maurice, ladies, gentleman, astronauts, and the entire world."

"I have to reply that while we have arguably over two hundred countries leaders here, and only nine of those that possess nuclear weapons, I bring the sad news that six of us are still not convinced."

"The aliens are not truthful in the reasoning behind us disarming the only weapon we could deploy against them in an intergalactic war."

"If there was only a way of them reassuring what their purpose is here, and if they are nurturing us to become equal to them over the generations, it all hinges on the belief in the Starsoul."

"If there is only a way, we could see these Starsouls in action, I am sure we would all be aboard."

Maurice confers with his fellow astronauts, and conferring smiles appeared across their faces.

Maurice came back to the microphone and said, "What you have said and asked Mr. President, is music to our ears."

"The Soulfurians are so intelligent, they have anticipated the response from you, and prepared a show for all mankind to see."

Just then all these blue lasers came out of the Soulfurian spaceship, docked above the International space station.

The blue lasers were directed into Earth's atmosphere. As the atmosphere was being saturated with this blue glow from all the Soulfurian lasers, there they were. The billions of billions of Starsouls were roaming the atmosphere.

Billions were pushing the wind and clouds; you could see them rising from the lands and going back down to the planet's surface. They were moving in perfect harmony. They were little ghostly spirits infused with cosmic energy.

The entire world was witnessing the purpose of Starsouls, and as time went on the blue lasers saturated all the air in the streets.

Everywhere you looked you could see these Starsouls.

The world's population went wide mouthed and silent. The President and his constituents were speechless.

Maurice then said, "This is what we have been witnessing throughout the cosmos, the galaxies, and solar systems. Every planet we visited contained these Starsouls."

"This was when we learned Starsouls energize the cosmos."

The President then said, "Let us all witness this revelation, and believe that the aliens are here to make us disarm these world destructing weapons. I ask of the other five leaders to lay down their nuclear arms and sign the accord."

He then confirmed that by asking a raise of hands from all nine countries with nuclear weapons, and in unanimous fashion all nine including the U.S. President had their hands up in unity. Instantly the world was rejoicing and dancing in the streets.

The astronauts were all hugging each other. Finally, for the first time the astronauts believed they were going home. Everyone in the world was happy all the leaders agreed.

They were drawing up The Nuclear Disarmament Accord for all nine nuclear countries to sign. As they were signing, there was an alarm from the space station.

All the astronauts had concerned looks on their faces as Maurice was calling to the president. "Mr. President, Mr. President we have a problem!"

The President answered "Maurice, please relax young man, we are all signing the accord as we speak." "That is the problem, said Maurice."

"The Soulfurian leader just informed us that the deal is off."

The Russian President grabbed the microphone, and questioned Maurice in English translation he said, "What do they mean the deal is off?

Do they know who their messing with? What good is their word if they can't keep an agreement?"

Maurice replies; "The Soulfurian said that the Nuclear Disarmament Accord is worded to include all nations with nuclear arms to agree to dismantle them.

"The Egyptian Leader replied, "All nine countries that possess nuclear weapons are signing the accord."

Maurice replied with, "When the Soulfurians flooded our atmosphere with the blue lasers to expose the Starsoul energies, it also exposed all the nuclear energy all over the world. It also exposed nuclear energies being secretly harbored in countries not in the nine signing the accord."

"This infuriated the Soulfurians, showing that even during a peace accord with them, there are still unbalanced Starsouls planning to ruin the agreement, and undermine the whole process."

The Chinese leader questioned, "Other countries?" "Who are these other countries among us that are ruining this plan for peace? Please expose them, and let us handle them, and let this peace agreement commence."

Maurice replied with, "The Soulfurians feel that if all you superpower nations, with all your spy technology cannot find this problem out for yourselves, then there is no hope for eternal peace between your countries. That implies nuclear war is unavoidable between your nations soon."

"The Soulfurians claim they are the keepers of Starsouls on this planet and all planets, and they will decide the fate of the human race, to cleanse the human race of unbalanced Starsouls, the way they have done in the past."

"They condemn this planet that is controlled by unbalanced Starsouls and give all of the human leader's fair warning to arm all of your I.C.B.M.s, and wait for the onslaught of asteroids and meteors."

"Just hope you have enough weapons to fight off the constant bombardment. They said they would give twenty-four hours to prepare your nations."

"The Soulfurians claim that their ultimate goal is to rid this world of nuclear weapons, and unbalanced Starsoul leaders."

"They will start their ultimate transformation of Earth, to a future Soulfurian planet from scratch. That means, this may be the equivalent to a human apocalypse."

"The Soulfurians recommend for all mankind to get their Starsouls balanced because their bodies may perish any day."

"Well, when humankind has their backs put against the wall, we can unite together, and overcome any attack by a non-human species."

"We will put our differences aside, and unite to show the biggest defense, and attack force this world has ever seen."

The Israeli leader finished his response with "Never underestimate the human race."

All the world leaders vowed to each other at the United Nations building in New York to stick together to fight these aliens till the end.

Then shortly after that, they all dispersed back to their native countries to lead their people. This was a time in the world for the masses of humanity, to look to their leaders for guidance.

Meanwhile on the International Space Station, the twelve astronauts were in a closed-door meeting with the Leader Soulfurian.

Everyone is assuming they could deal an agreement with the aliens, and for them to divert an all-out massacre of the human population on Earth.

The world's population was in fear, as the two giant forces were about to square off.

There were the millions of alien spacecraft around the asteroid belt in the solar system, and about three thousand ICBM nuclear rockets, land and submarine based.

They were getting ready to be launched by the big three countries of The United States, Russia and China.

The next day after the meeting between the astronauts and the Soulfurian leader, the astronauts appeared back on live feed from the International Space Station.

Adam gets on the microphone and announces to the entire world's masses,

"We have just finished a meeting with The Soulfurian leader, and they recommend all Soulfuturans, that means you, need to stay inside and keep your TV's on, as we will be in communication with you through this whole ordeal."

"They will be giving us their intentions as we are to relay them to the leaders. They say you are about to see the greatest laser, and fireworks show this world has ever seen.

"This is Commander John A Leonard of the United States Air Force Space Defense division. I am here on the orders of the Oval office to keep communication lines open to all of you astronauts while we prepare for operation N.A.T.O. Shield."

"This is a worldwide defense system in place where all nuclear nations are working hand in hand with protecting our planet from an alien attack."

Maurice grabs the microphone, "Mr. Leonard, with all due respect, these are not just aliens. These are Soulfurians from planet Soulfuria we have visited twice."

"It is a more advanced society with absolutely no violence. The time has come when all the militaries of our world, have met their match. You will see how ineffective your weaponry is outside this world's boundaries."

"You will find how powerful the Soulfurians can become. Do you realize everything we know to this date; they have learned millions of years before this?

Mankind can try to defend, but whatever the outcome, the Soulfurians will be the victor."

"The Soulfurians are our Starsoul keepers, which mean they can see if our Starsouls are imbalanced, and they could eliminate any evil created by unbalanced Starsouls."

"Those evils they are focused on right now are all the nuclear weapons of the world. Or they can just eliminate all imbalanced Starsouls from the planet. We do not know which of the two methods they will choose."

Commander Leonard, "Well, I guess we will just have to wait and see. What I need from you is all your cooperation and intel, of when the Soulfurians are planning to attack. Also, you being a part of U.S. military personnel that is an order! Do you understand Mr. Kālu?"

"Yes Sir," replied Maurice.

Just as Maurice was communicating with U.S. Space command, so was every other astronaut with their countries Space Commands. The Communications were open with the astronauts, and the world's militaries.

The whole world was anxiously waiting what the Soulfurians would do.

It was time, exactly twenty-four hours later, and the assault from the skies has started.

First it was laser beams, and they were coming from every direction from above. Because it was nighttime, it looked like a laser show.

Thousands of red lasers were beaming down to Earth, but people did not know where they were going.

People flocked to their T.V.'s to see if the Astronauts had any answers.

"This is Commander Leonard, calling Lieutenant Commander Kālu; can you read me Mr. Kālu?"

"I am right here Commander Leonard, how can I help you?"

"I am getting reports from all over our country, and also our neighboring countries, that they are methodically destroying all our ground-based nuclear stockpiles with these lasers. They are burning holes in the weapons making them useless. Tell them they must stop those lasers or else."

"Or else, Commander Leonard?" "Yes, they tell us to tell you that when they filled our atmosphere with blue lasers, their computers tracked every stockpile of nuclear weapons in the world. And for the next eight hours they will destroy them."

"If you try to move them from their positions, you risk yourself from being hit by one of those deadly lasers, and there's absolutely nothing we can do about it."

The Commander continued "We demand that they stop this assault on the world's weapon supply."

The Russian communications to Dmitri S. Federoff with China's Supreme command communicating with Zhang K. Chen were all saying the same thing.

How these lasers from space were ruining all their ground base stockpiles of nuclear weapons. This same result is being reported all over the world in countries like Iran, North Korea, Pakistan, India and Israel, The nuclear weapons out in the open air are game for these precise lasers.

The world's militaries just must sit back and watch as their nuclear stockpile weapons are being destroyed. These lasers are coming from every direction from the skies, and they know exactly where every stockpile nuclear weapon in the world is located.

With the news that the Soulfurians were targeting only nuclear stockpiles, it was music to the world's masses ears. Also, that it will continue for the next eight hours, brought people from their hiding places. There were people gathering at their old familiar spots like Time Square, and other video streaming places around the world. The news also gave people a sense of mercy on the general people at least for the next eight hours, hearing they were targeting military institutions only.

They were coming outside to watch the greatest light, and laser show they ever saw. The people watched as the lasers hit their targets. There was footage of the destruction all over the internet, and news media.

Little did the masses realize, they were watching something they never saw, and they were watching the biggest militaries all over the world take weapons from them, without one drop of human blood. This was truly a miracle they were witnessing.

It made the crowds believe in the Soulfurians, and what they had to teach the human race.

A non-violent confrontation was the best answer to any confrontation.

It was one hour into the Soulfurian assault on nuclear stockpiles, when suddenly everyone was listening to Eve talking to Adam.

Eve said to Adam, "Maybe this whole Starsoul way of living is the truth like the Soulfurians are telling us.

Just maybe the only thing that matters to us are our Starsouls and how we live our lives. Did you ever look at it that way?"

"If we believe that living a balanced and a good life would make us live eternally, and have our Starsouls live with all the energies of our planet, then there would be no fear of death and sadness over loved ones that passed. We would know they are free as our free-spirited atmosphere."

Adam replied, "Yes it would be a very bad decision to think killing another human would get you a rewarded afterlife."

"When it really frees the Starsoul of the person you are killing, and it would condemn your Starsoul to be extinguished in a fiery hell with our host Star."

Boy would that be a shocker." "My thoughts would ask, if we are the great, great grandparents to future Soulfurians, are we really evolving into them?"

Maurice intervenes with, "Guys and gals, we are being broadcasted worldwide, we cannot let our personal thoughts and questions be broadcasted for the entire world to hear. Let's keep our personal beliefs to ourselves, for it takes a world of different beliefs to make the world go around."

The two answered, "Sorry Lieutenant, and sorry world, we were unaware our microphones were on.

They were just our personal thoughts, and it had no place for this public forum."

Just then the astronauts could hear the world cheering all the way from the space station.

Adam says to Eve in his "John Wayne" voice, "I think we lassoed them back on our side again."

Eve then replied, "Adam they never left." Then the crowds were going crazy yelling Starsouls! Starsouls! Starsouls!

Commander Leonard broke in, "I hate to steal the limelight from you guys, but you need to tell those aliens to stop the laser attack. We all agree to sign an accord to dismantle all nuclear weapons."

"What they are doing in place is depleting our weapon supplies, leaving our country vulnerable to other countries just walking in and taking us over. This is absurd!"

Maurice replied, "Commander, the Soulfurians are telling us that what is happening to your weapons is happening to everyone else's nuclear weapons."

"They are making an even playing field to ensure future disagreement between your countries would be settled with pen, paper, and a handshake."

"Rather than rattling nuclear threats at each other. They said, just six more hours, and they will be halfway finished of what they are set out to do."

"The Soulfurians also said, "It's great to see all the world's militaries, working together for a cause. It's the first time in human history that something like that has happened."

The Commander replied, "Now how would they know that?"

Maurice replied,"They know everything, they have been watching, and shaping us into developing Soulfurians since the beginning of time. Do you think all the technology advances came from thin air? Do you believe all the inventions of our world were pure genius?

Well, they came from human minds that obtained advanced Soulfurian Starsouls, which is another term for genius."

The laser attack was relentless, with every military base being affected from China to the United States. There were media shots of whole military bases stockpiles turned into stockpiles of metal scrap.

"The World's Response"

Israel's nuclear weapons were almost gone while countries like Iran, and North Korea who were just developing nukes, were completely wiped out of all nuclear weapons. The big three would take some time to deplete their stock of weapons that ran into the thousands.

Commander Leonard says to Maurice, "We are a little skeptical over what these aliens stand for, and their motive here. They gave us an ultimatum for all of us to sign the accord. Once we agreed to that they said no deal and gave an excuse about other nations harboring nukes. Well, it looks like they just got rid of those nation's nukes."

"So why are they still going forth with this campaign of lasers up our asses? I'll tell you why, we were right thinking they just want to eliminate the one weapon that can stop them from total invasion of their spaceships."

"That's it, isn't it? They plan to take over this planet. That's what your video showed, when it showed an ape skull looking basically the same for 34 million of years, and in a few million years it transforms to a human skull. It shows the evolution of our human bodies over the centuries losing hair, earlobes and mouths shrinking. With our heads growing balder and bigger, and fingertips swelling on the tips, then it shows us thousands of years from now looking like they do today."

"The whole story was to show them taking over, and we are now on to their scheme. We have a State of the Union Address coming up from the President of The United States, and he will lay the law down for these aliens."

Maurice replies to the commander, "Ok we will just wait for the President to speak."

Eve turns to Charles Jones, the British astronaut and says, "They just don't get what the Soulfurians want do they?"

Charles replies, "No, I guess they don't, I guess down there on the ground, it's a little hard to stand up for world peace. We have been doing that with these Soulfurians for over a year now."

"The Soulfurians have been nothing but peaceful and teaching us peace is our salvation."

"Even during these laser strikes all over the world, they haven't touched or killed one human in doing it. All our leaders want, is to look beyond the good they are doing, and respond with aggression. I just don't get it. Will there ever be peace in our lifetime or the lifetime of our children?'

It's been five hours, and the only three countries the Soulfurians are focusing their lasers on right now, are China, Russia and the U.S. They have double the lasers doing the damage on these countries' nuclear stockpiles, since they finished the other countries by this time.

The media was at every military base in the United States showing on TV, shared on social media, and put in every living room in America.

The undeniable elimination of nuclear stockpiles of weapons. All the other non-nuclear weapons they were leaving alone.

People were demonstrating in every city street in America for these Soulfurians, after seeing what they were doing. It gave the people a sense of security, they were focusing on the weapons only. Others stayed bunkered down in their houses waiting for a full out alien invasion.

No one knows what the Soulfurians have in store for them. It is now in the eighth hour, and the lasers are finishing up on the nuclear weapon meltdown.

The President of the United States is about to make the State of the Union Address. The news reporter announced, "Ladies and Gentlemen, here is our President of the United States."

All the people in the States found their way to a video outlet, or a T.V. screen at the local pub to listen in.

"Good Evening Ladies and gentlemen of this great nation, and to all the great nations on this planet.

We have been put in a place in time and history, that no man or woman has been before. The last day especially has been harrowing for our military."

"We have been under attack by these Soulfurians, or aliens as our astronauts would refer to them as. Let's go back to the beginning, a little over one year ago, when our combined astronauts from our country, and all countries of the world went into space for a mission of peace."

"Well, peace was the last thing they were thinking about when they were violently ripped from their lifelines, while being tethered in space by a cable, and vacuumed up like they were a few nuts and bolts, being sucked up by a giant shop vac. So that makes one strike against the Soulfurians at this point."

"Then they took them away on a trip as you all seen in the video. Explaining to and showing them various worlds that were never witnessed before by humans."

"They taught them from their account, how we evolved on this great Earth, by controlling a source of energy called a Starsoul. An interesting theory, I must admit."

"That would be a nice story to brainwash our astronauts and concoct a grand plan to invade us. Also, they were keeping the astronauts captive as prisoners of war, away from their families for a whole year against their will."

"That would make strike two against these Soulfurian aliens. Would you not agree? I would think not!"

"Then they brought them home after, by the way we spent ten million dollars building this communication beacon with a message to bring them home and help guide them back here."

"So, I will give the Soulfurians the benefit of the doubt, that they had good intentions by bringing them back."

"I will take one strike back for that, just leaving them with one strike. Ok, now our astronauts are back, or are they? The Soulfurians will not let us near the International Space Station to meet our astronauts, after not seeing them for a year, and a year of thinking the worst of their fates."

"They still have them brainwashed up in space, being held against their will. For that fact, they get their second strike back. Now they give them a set of laws to give to us to live by".

"To tell you the truth, if these aliens were legit, and for real, it would not be a bad plan to live by."

"What I believe is, they gave them laws to brainwash us. Even that is not a major infraction in the real world, they had a couple of great points."

"What they really did was threaten us to live by these laws, or they would wipe out the whole human race, with asteroid pounding on our planet, like they said they did with the dinosaurs in the past."

"Then on top of that, after we agreed to sign this Nuclear Disarmament Accord, they reneged on their half of the agreement."

Or should I say threatened, and attacked every country's military, by all country's rules of engagement say, this is an aggressive act of war. That would be strike three ladies and gentlemen."

"This is no ordinary act of war on a Province or Nation."

"This is an act of war against humanity. An alien force is threatening to kill us all on this planet and has already shown they can very well do that."

"You know these Soulfurians are very good at brainwashing, but I am here to bring you all back to reality."

"If we do not act, and protect our world, then we have failed ourselves. These aliens have put us in a position of no turning back."

"I was elected to this great nation as Commander and Chief. The first thing a Commander and Chief will do in a time of war is to check with his generals of each military division. But the stakes are much higher than that on this front. So, the first thing I did was check with the other Commander and Chiefs of the world."

"We had a three-hour satellite conference call between all of the world powers, and we unanimously decided on a solution to this human crisis."

"As you know, the aliens depleted all the world's stockpiles of nuclear weapons. Most were short range weapons."

"Weapons we could have used against them if they came down here to invade."

"Because they took those weapons off the playing field, it gives us a strong feeling they plan to come down and invade."

"The one ace in our sleeve we have, is weapons that can wipe them out before they get to us."

"These weapons are hidden all over the world. They are hidden underground, and in submarines, in ships in the seas all over the world. These weapons are the ones the aliens could not detect when they were fooling us by exposing these Starsouls, when really they were hunting down our weapons."

These are weapons the aliens called us out on, when they were giving us their warnings. These weapons are long range I.C.B.M.'s, which stands for Inter-Continental Ballistic Missiles."

"These weapons are designed to fly into space and then re-enter halfway across the world in another country. There are about four thousand between land and seas, possessed by the three superpower countries."

"These are spread out throughout the world. These babies pack a punch that I'll bet these aliens never witnessed in their millions of years of existence."

"Now our scientist and space observatories have been monitoring these alien starships, and they are numbered by the millions, all along the solar system's asteroid belt. For those of you not familiar with the term asteroid belt, it is a ring around our solar system between Mars and Jupiter."

"It comprises large rock, ice and metals that if any of these were directed at us, could be catastrophic for our planet."

"Every day common meteors fall to our planet, but they are insignificant and widespread throughout our planet. Then there are comets. These projectiles are made of ice and could do significant damage if landed in the right area."

"Just to give you an idea how big asteroids are, they are gigantic compared to a comet. Some of these can be as large as six miles wide."

"These aliens are threatening us with these asteroids. They are claiming to be cleansing our world of unbalanced Starsouls to end our existence."

"We will not take this laying down. The three-nation pact has decided to initiate an all-out ballistic attack on these alien ships, hiding around the asteroid belt. We have enough firepower the blow the whole asteroid belt away into space, and in the process taking every alien spaceship out also."

"With no further ado, I am signing an executive order for all branches of our military to prepare for war with this alien force, willing to inflict harm on our world. My constituents in China and Russia are doing the same, and the three of us are working, and communicating in unison on this mission."

"Also, we will have the help and resources of fifteen other nations with radar and guidance systems. I will now say goodnight to you all, and just remember your military and all the militaries of this world are here to protect you."

The President walked away, and an advisor to the president was fielding questions from the reporters.

"Hello, my name is Carl Herzberg, I am the president's advisor, and I will answer a brief number of questions from the crowd."

"Ok you, young man in the blue shirt, go ahead." "Hello, this is Ryan Metcalf of the Florida Sun Times, my question to the administration, is it true that all the world's militaries are working together on this?"

Carl, "Yes the truth is, this is the first time in history that there are these amounts of militaries all over the world conducting joint military operations. Carl," You over there, in the Jeff hat, go ahead."

"Hello, Mr. Herzberg, my name is Richard Alverez from the Times Herald in Boston Mass."

"My question is if all these nations start blowing apart the asteroid belt, what kinds of backlash will that have on us environmentally?"

"Carl, "Thanks for asking." The asteroid belt is millions of miles from Earth. Even when they launch the rockets, they are not certain they all will reach the belt."

"This has never been attempted before. I would think the powers to be, have calculated all the possible scenarios, and I'm sure the world's minds would not have come up with this plan if it posed any danger to Earth."

Carl, "Ok next, you the young lady over there, you can go."

"Hello, my name is Stephanie Manger, of the Reno County Journal, my question would be, how much time will it take to get this operation together, and how long will the operation be?"

Carl, "We know they are putting everything in motion as we speak. There is a real sense of urgency here because we know as soon as the President laid out our plan, the aliens will be doing something to counter."

"That's why it is imperative that everyone takes cover during this time. The aliens could start to deflect those asteroids at us right now for a preemptive strike."

"Ok, I have time for one more question, how about you, nice gentleman with the suspenders on in the second row to the right of me."

"Well, thank you Sir, I am Willy Netcaf, from the Louisiana Bog County Gazette, and I am here to question, how the hell are we supposed to believe that sending rockets into outer space millions of miles away, we are going to get lucky enough to hit alien spaceships?"

Carl, "Well Mr. Netcalf, these rockets are so powerful, I believe they can destroy all the alien ships, and the asteroid belt in one shot."

"Our military experts also share the same belief. Ok, that will end our session, and thank you all for coming out tonight."

As soon as the conference ended, the video screens around the world came alive with transmission from the International space station. It was Adam on the screen, and he had a look on his face of fear.

He shouted to the world, "IT WON'T WORK," TELL YOUR LEADERS, IT WON'T WORK."

"The Soulfurians heard your plan, and they said it would be foolish for our leaders to try such a plan."

"They said, even your best nuclear weapons would not be powerful enough to destroy them. They said, once again millions of lives are going to be wasted on the decision of a few cosmically unbalanced Starsouls."

"People of the world, take shelter, there will be a rain of asteroids, comets and meteors to come shortly."

"The Soulfurians are going ahead with their regeneration plan, and it will wipe out ninety percent of life on Earth."

"They were considering other options, until they heard the aggressive attack the world's militaries were about to take on them. They say the days of unbalanced Starsouls, leading the fate of millions must come to an end. The Soulfurians say to take shelter, you may be part of the lucky ten percent that will live, to see a new day of a world in peace. May God bless all of your Starsouls."

The world prepares for the biggest battle the Earth has ever seen. Every man, woman, and child found shelter in the places they figured would be their final resting places. Families were united.

Places of worship were jammed to the max. It was a grim time, as the world was waiting to die. There was not much they could do. The two sides made their final decisions.

There was no option of peace. People just accepted the grim outcome, and hoped they would be in the spared ten percent of survivors.

Some had their last meals, and went off to sleep, hoping tomorrow would bring a better outcome, and the Soulfurians would have mercy on them. People thought it was ironic that the very aliens that brought world peace would bring world destruction.

"The Answer"

The twelve astronauts felt deserted by these aliens promising a land of peace, and being suspended hopelessly, knowing that all their families below on Earth were about to perish.

It was six o' clock am. The stage was set. The United States had their nuclear submarines stationed in the Gulf of Mexico, North Atlantic Ocean, South Atlantic Ocean, Arctic Ocean, and Pacific Ocean. They had all the I.C.B.M.'s in launch ready mode, in just about every State in America, and South America.

The Chinese had their nuclear Submarines in the Pacific Ocean, Indian Ocean, Arctic Ocean, and Southern Ocean. Also, they had their I.C.B.M. rockets in launch ready mode in every area of Asia.

The Russian's had their nuclear submarines spread out in all oceans mentioned above. Also, they have their nuclear I.C.B.M's locked and loaded readily to go.

The President of the United States was stationed at a world space observatory. Haleakala Observatory in Maui Hawaii was the location, while the other world leaders were at various space observatories throughout the world. The observatory was set as a temporary military command center. The whole island was guarded off by military police, and the place was crawling with C.I.A. personnel.

There was military housing built by the core of engineers on the grounds. The President and his staff were flown in by helicopter. There was radio antennas erected, and satellite dishes installed for communications.

Who would guess, after the technology boom in the last ten years that the President of the United States, and all of his security must rely on the necessities of life in the time of a galactic war?

The president was acquainted with the lead space observer, as he and his Chief of Staff were briefed on how to observe the main space telescope.

The President was in direct contact with the Chinese and Russian Leaders, as they were also stationed at observatories. The President's Chief of Staff was in direct contact with the four branches of the military, who was on standby waiting for the Presidents orders.

"You see Mr. President, just look into that telescope, and you can see the asteroid belt.

The President, "Yes I see it now."

Observer, "Now see those odd round silver discs that are standing out from the rocks?"

The President, "Yes there seems to be a lot of them, I thought they were chunks of ice."

Observer, "No Mr. President, they are alien spacecraft. We have been observing them for the last twelve hours."

"They are just hovering, and switching positions every hour or two. They have not left for any refueling or anything. I wonder what they are powered with."

The President, "Maybe after we blow a couple out of commission, we might get lucky and a couple might fall back to Earth. We could retrieve them from the ocean. Get me on the Phone with China and Russia."

"I need a three-way conference call right now." Chief of Staff, "Ok sir, we're working on it right now." A few minutes later the President was in a conference with the Chinese and Russian leaders.

The President, "Hey guys are you seeing what I am seeing?"

Russian leader, "Yes those aliens hiding behind those rocks."

China Leader, "We must strike first. It will take 12 hours to reach their targets."

President, "Yes it is time to launch a preemptive strike."

Russian Leader, "Yes let's set it for a thirty-minute countdown launch."

China Leader, "Ok, let's start the countdown now."

President, "Thank you fellows, I will give the go ahead now with a launch in thirty minutes." The three leaders agreed, as the President hung up the phone.

The President turned to his Chief of Staff and ordered the launch.

The Chief of Staff called all the branches of the U.S. Military, and gave the order to launch in thirty minutes. The news traveled fast as the media was hungry for information.

The headlines read "Armageddon," streets were abandoned.

Looting was running rampant, as all stores were closed. People were trying to get anything they could to use for survival. It was an eerie time in the world.

The news circled the globe of a thirty-minute strike. The news drew curious people out to watch as they never saw nuclear rockets launched.

They were gathering on mountain tops, and anywhere along the coastline to get a glimpse.

It was time T -30 seconds, as the onlookers were anxiously waiting, 29,28,27,26,25,24,23,22,21,20,19,18,

17,16,15,14,13,12,11,TEN, NINE, EIGHT, SEVEN, SIX,FIVE, FOUR, THREE, TWO, ONE,

There they went, all around the world from land and sea. There were thousands of I.C.B.M.'s jutting up through the atmosphere.

It was such an emotional event, it brought millions of onlookers to their knees praying and sobbing.

The world knew it would never be the same, even knowing the rockets were headed to the far reaches of space. The news also spread; it would take the rockets twelve hours to reach the asteroid belt.

That would set the demolition for around 9:00pm. EST.

Meanwhile at the I.S.S, the twelve astronauts were working diligently in negotiations with the Soulfurian leader on an alternative ending. It was a closed meeting that was not broadcasted to the world.

The President was in observation of the track the nuclear rockets were taking.

He questioned his advisors if the rockets had enough fuel to last the trip?

His advisors told him the rockets will run out of fuel about halfway there.

They also said, once they have the inertia of speed with no gravity to slow them down, they will be free flying on a one-way trip until they hit the target. All the thousands of I.C.B.M.'s were now in space headed to the asteroid belt.

The President was in conference with other leaders, and they all had their eyes on the alien spacecraft.

It was just a waiting game of when the aliens would leave or deflect asteroids to Earth. The three leaders knew if the latter scenario happened, whatever asteroids made it past, the oncoming rockets, would be free falling to the earth, with no defense against them. This made the President on edge, as time went on for the rockets to reach their targets.

It was two hours later, and nothing has changed. The Soulfurian spaceships were still in the asteroid belt by the millions.

The I.C.B.M.'s were still ten hours away. The president was in question with the other leaders of why the aliens have not made a counter move. The President knew they were dealing with an intelligent foe, with millions of years of experience with technology.

It has been six hours now, and still there has been no move in the chess match between the two forces. The nuclear bombs were still on target, and they were running out of fuel.

The President was trying to strive to reach communication with the I.S.S, to see if the astronauts had any inside information on the alien's intentions.

There was a cutoff of communication between The I.S.S., and the rest of the world by the Soulfurian force. It was now getting dark in the Eastern Time zone. It was about 8:00pm Eastern Standard Time, and the president was called by his space observer, there was movement with the alien spaceships.

The President went to the phone with the other leaders, as they all looked through a telescope, and witnessed the Soulfurian spaceships pulling back from the asteroid belt and disappearing further into space. The three leaders were in disgust, and cursing up a storm, knowing that their rockets could not pass the asteroid belt to get the alien ships.

Right away things looked grim for the human leaders, as their imaginations were running rampant about them looking like fools when the aliens come down to invade.

Knowing they just threw away their only weapons to stop the aliens. The President, the Russian, and China leaders were played by the Soulfurians by the old bait and switch trick. There was nothing they can do, as the first of the nuclear explosions started. It started with a few, then suddenly, it looked like a grand finale in a firework display in space.

There was explosion after explosion of rocks and matter exploding in every direction.

You could even see the destruction from the ground, and the echoes of such explosions were chilling. The explosions went on for an hour, and it seemed like a year.

As the space observatories around the world were watching the same thing, the country's leaders were watching. There was a frightening new event unfolding as the explosions were ending.

The aftermath of the explosions caused the asteroids to blow into smaller pieces, and millions of smaller pieces were heading back towards Earth. Everyone panicked. All the leaders, and the people of Earth were in complete fear.

The Soulfurians tricked the human leaders into doing what they threatened they would do. That very thing the humans tried to stop is what they caused themselves.

Thousands of Comets and Earth destructing meteors headed straight towards Earth, with nothing stopping them.

The President held an emergency State of the Union Address to the U.S., and the world right from the grounds on the island.

The President was short and to the point. He started with "Ladies and gentlemen, and children all across the world."

" We have done everything in our power to protect you, and we have failed. You have our deepest apologies, and what is important is to take shelter."

"In a matter of one hour from now, we will be bombarded all over the world with Earth destroying projectiles of all size, and diameter."

"It will be too much for us to handle, and for those who survive will die a slow death from years of dust clouds blocking the sun. It is time to stop talking, and be with a loved one, and pray for one final time. Goodnight."

As the President was walking away waiting for the inevitable to happen one of his aides nudged him on the shoulder and said,

"Mister President Lookup, they are here!"

The President walked outside, and looked up to the sky. Low and behold the whole sky was covered with giant round Soulfurian spacecraft.

From east to west and north to south, there were millions of spacecrafts covering the night sky.

The President walked down the steps looking until he walked to the middle of the road, and yelled up,

"WHAT DO YOU WANT WITH US NOW?"

Just then the transmission from the I.S.S. appeared on every video screen in the world. A secret service car pulled up as the President jumped in to view the TV. Monitor in the car.

It was of all people Adam, and all he said was, "Our Space Angels are here to the rescue."

When everyone heard those words from Adam, they started outside all teary-eyed of joy looking up in the sky, as they saw millions of Soulfurian spacecraft shooting green lasers up into space. Billions of laser beams protected planet Earth from incoming debris. The lasers were too much for the incoming comets and meteors as they were being pulverized to dust in space by the alien lasers.

The President called to Maurice, and Maurice replied with, "Yes Mister President."

"Mission Commander Maurice, please tell me why the Soulfurians are saving us right now, and not invading or wiping us out?"

Maurice, "You see Mr. President, over a year ago we went to space for a cause, and that cause was world peace.

The Soulfurians heard our cry and showed us worlds made up with nothing but world peace. They took us to their home planet to show us how a world lives in peace."

'They also showed us something else Mr. President, they showed us the meaning of life as we know it."

"They showed us this energy inside of us that is also in every living thing. It is the reason we exist. It is the energy of this universe, and galaxy. This energy inside of us is special, and we should treat it special by living a life of peace."

"The Soulfurians did not want to meddle with the evolution of man once they started it."

"They managed to rid our world of all nuclear weapons, and most of all they managed to get every country that was rattling sabers at each other, to work together for a cause, and get the whole world together as one."

"They never wanted to harm us all along. We are their future generations, and they will do anything necessary to protect us."

"Yes, Mr. President they are truly our Space Angels." "All they ask is for us to believe in the Starsoul way of life. They want us to carry on and live in peace."

"After they are finished cleaning up the mess we made in space, they are moving on to fix other issues in the cosmos and prepare their planet for nirvana."

"They said, they will be back here to live for good when we eventually evolve into their kind. Until then, have a peaceful life and prosper Mr. President."

The President then opened his car door and stepped outside to see the show the Soulfurians were putting on.

"Wait Mr. President, they just contacted me, and they want to show us one more time the existence of Starsouls before they leave us."

Just then purple lasers shining downed from the Soulfurian spaceships.

The President asked, "What are these purple lasers for, and where are they going?"

Maurice answered, "They told me they are shining on all the dying humans in the world right now, the humans that are dying in hospitals, hospices, and even people getting killed by accident as we speak."

"When they pass away, their loved ones by their sides will witness their Starsouls leaving their bodies and traveling up and joining the atmosphere."

Just then you could hear the echoes of joy, and happiness all over the world in the air of all the relatives, and friends of dying loved ones.

Just then the President looked up in the sky, and the words, "BELIEVE IN THE STARSOULS" was spelled out by the Soulfurian starships as they slowly faded in the night sky.

After the Soulfurians had left our skies, and human life went on. There were space flights to the International Space Station to pick up the twelve astronauts, and label them the "Real World Heroes."

All twelve astronauts were brought back to their home countries, and there were celebrations, and ticker tape parades, with the Space Heroes perched upon a throne in the parades.

From that point on, the world continued the Starsouls belief, resulting in total world peace. There was a 'One World Order" made up that met at the International Space Station twice a year. They virtually ruled the world with the influence of all nations.

The twelve astronauts continued their careers as intelligence agents with their home governments on technology, and information using their lifelong talent of telepathy to communicate with the Soulfurian world.

THE END

TWO POEMS FROM THE AUTHOR

Taken away into the vast space,
  one giant step for the human race.
  Shown the origin world of our past,
it was a place of peace and ever last.
A world with no evil and no one sad,

what a wonderful world is what we had.
Until evil entered and thrust us away,
to the blue world we live in today.

New babies born and graduations,
to a busy life of trial and tribulations.
Once we learn to rid our souls of Satin,
our life here ends as our spaceship's waiting.
To take our souls back into the vast space
to the origin world of a perfect alien race.

WHAT IS IT?

It is made of calcium, magnesium and sodium,

If you guessed a bag of ice melt, we are not done.

It is also made of hydrogen and oxygen,

If you guessed a raindrop, you're not the only one.

It is also comprised of phosphorus and potassium.

If you guessed plant food, I'll give you another clue.

It is made of sulfur, chlorine and carbon.

If you guessed table salt, that's not totally true.

All these elements, that originate from a Star.

With the energy from the star its driving force,

to keep all these elements together of course.

So, what is this cosmic science project we have here?

A body of elements powered by a soul.

Just look in a mirror, and smile from ear to ear.

It is your human body all together as a whole.